Silver Dreams

Silver
Dreams

Kate Moseman

Silver Dreams

Copyright © 2021 by Kate Moseman

All rights reserved. No part of this book may be reproduced or used in any manner without written permission of the copyright owner except for the use of quotations in a book review.

This is a work of fiction. Names, characters, places, and incidents either are the product of the author's imagination or are used fictitiously. Any resemblance to actual persons, living or dead, events, or locales is entirely coincidental.

First Edition

ISBN 978-1-7345144-8-3 (ebook)
ISBN 978-1-7345144-9-0 (paperback)

Published by:
Fortunella Press

Sailing is like dancing with the wind.
Sometimes, she likes to cha-cha.

—Captain DJ McCabe, U-Sail of Central Florida

1

I wrapped my hand around the bathtub faucet opening in a desperate attempt to stop the water gushing out of it, but the water surged through my fingers anyway. "Knock it *off*," I said, concentrating my magic on reversing the flow. The water grumbled like a disobedient child and retreated into the pipes.

I let out a sigh of relief.

Then the toilet began to bubble.

I squeaked in dismay and released the tub faucet.

"Pepper?" my husband, Pete, called from outside the bathroom door. "You almost ready?"

"I'll be right there," I replied, as chipper as I could manage. I leaned over the misbehaving toilet water and tried to think calm thoughts. My curls dangled in my face. I spread my hands in the air above the seat and made a soothing motion.

The water burped and bubbled a few more times, then settled with one last silvery magical flash.

I sat on the edge of the tub and regarded the toilet with suspicion, but whatever it was had stopped.

Of course all of this would happen right when I was about to go on vacation. Lately my water magic had been getting a little . . . unruly. I could still call it up, move it around, make it do what I wanted—but sometimes it had a mind of its own, popping up when I least expected it from sinks, tubs, and now toilets.

I grabbed a towel and mopped up the water around the tub. Thank God the toilet water hadn't gotten high enough to splash.

I dropped the towel in the hamper and faced the mirror. My brown curls popped nicely, although they were a little frizzy thanks to the Florida humidity. My sporty casual shirt and favorite cargo shorts said *vacation*, but my face said *total freak-out*.

Maybe it was too much to ask to look carefree. I hadn't even left for vacation yet. I straightened the black Tahitian pearl on my leather necklace, picked up my purse, and gave the plumbing one last dark look before I opened the bathroom door.

Normally, the boys would have been sword fighting with pool noodles in the living room, but we'd dropped them off with my dad and stepmom earlier so we could finish getting packed and ready. Now Pete's electric razor made the only sound in the house.

We hadn't been alone with each other like this since before the kids were born.

Not that there was anything wrong. Just because you sometimes look at your spouse like they're a really good coworker doesn't mean things are going wrong.

Here was our chance to reconnect. I should have run through the house skipping for joy. Instead, I stuck my head in my oldest son's bedroom.

Rocky's room was a certified disaster area with clothes on the floor and an assortment of pencil sketches of castles stuck to the walls with tape. A dozen books of folktales teetered in a stack on his bedside table, topped with his favorite, *Stories from Old Russia*.

How much longer did we have before he gave up castles and folktales for something more grown-up?

My youngest boy's bedroom wasn't any neater. There were so many Legos on the floor it looked like a beach made of chunky multicolored sand. I carefully picked my way across the tiny patches of carpet to the edge of his twin bed. I gathered up a small tattered quilt and pressed it to my face.

He was way too big for me to pick up anymore, but he still liked to have his old baby blanket when he slept.

My husband poked his head in the doorway. Without the cover of his usual dentist's white coat, his vintage style was on full display: a retro shirt with geometric designs, thick black eyeglass frames, and a short-brimmed straw fedora. "Honey? Are you snuggling Kevin's baby blanket again?"

"Shut up. Don't even pretend you don't do it all the time." I balled up the blanket and threw it at him.

He caught it and pressed it to his cheek. Then he carefully crossed the room and smoothed the blanket over the end of the bed. Faded sailboats marched across the fabric.

The house was so very quiet.

Pete took my hand, gently, as if I might startle.

I leaned my head on his shoulder. "They're getting so big." I surveyed the empty room, vaguely sure that there was a reason I shouldn't leave. That I should go back and pick up the kids and cancel the whole thing.

What was wrong with me?

"They practically pushed us out the door when we dropped them off at your parents' house," said Pete.

I shook myself. I was the fun one. I shouldn't be moping in my kids' rooms when vacation called. "You're right. This is going to be the best vacation ever."

"That's my girl. Come on, it's check-in time." He moved toward the door and stepped on a Lego. "Ow! First thing when we get back, we're cleaning this up."

"Sure we will." Neither of us actually wanted to brave the horror of cleaning up all those Legos, but we did a good job of mutually procrastinating by claiming we'd do it soon.

That reminded me of my own to-do list: I still hadn't told Pete about my magic.

My friends had it easy. Luella and Rose were dating *literally* magical men.

My husband's a dentist.

Don't get me wrong—he's great. But that's a lot of explaining to do, and what if he didn't take it well?

We gathered our bags and hauled them out to the car. Pete loaded them in the trunk while I locked the front door.

He opened the passenger side door and made a sweeping, gallant gesture. "My lady," he said, "your chariot awaits."

I slid into the seat.

He closed the door and went around to the driver's side. He entered, buckled his seatbelt, glanced at his watch, adjusted the mirrors, checked his black-and-silver hair in the mirror, and wrapped his hands around the wheel.

He hadn't pushed the ignition button, though.

"Pete?"

He stared straight ahead.

The only thing in front of us was the garage door.

"Pete, are you okay?"

"Hmm? Oh, yeah, I'm okay." He pushed the ignition button, then continued to just sit there.

"Did you want to go, or shall we spend our vacation in the driveway?"

"You think the kids will be okay?"

I snorted. "It's not just me, then."

He took one hand off the wheel to make a dismissive gesture. "They'll be fine." He sounded like he was trying to convince himself as much as he was trying to convince me.

I did a shoulder shimmy—the best dance move I could manage while buckled in my seat. "Vivacqua Resort, here we come!"

An awkward silence fell as we backed out of the driveway and made our way out of our neighborhood. The familiar buildings of Sparkle Beach whipped by. "So," I said. "What do you want to talk about?"

"We can talk about . . ." His hand groped the air like he might find a conversational topic floating in it. "Politics!"

"Ugh."

"No, wait—I have a work story I forgot to tell you!"

I grimaced. As an accountant, my work stories involved math. His work stories involved teeth. Neither one made for sparkling conversation.

"Don't make that face. It's a good one."

"Fine, tell me your work story."

He settled happily into driving-while-storytelling mode, one hand on the wheel and the other meandering through the air while he talked. "So this lady comes in the other day—"

"Age?"

"Retired, probably. Anyway, she comes in complaining of a loose crown. No insurance. Insists she'll pay cash."

I stifled a sigh. A tooth story.

"So I get it all fixed up. She's ready to go. She goes up to the desk to pay, and—get this—she hands over a bunch of gold coins!"

"Gold coins?"

"The office ladies don't know what to do, so they call me over. I say, 'Ma'am, I'm sorry, but we don't accept gold coins as a form of payment.' And *she* says, 'It's gold coins or nothing, sonny. Take it or leave it.' I look at the coins on the desk—gold's probably running fifteen hundred an ounce—and figure, what the heck? I took it."

"You *took* it?"

"I took it." He stuck his hand in his pocket and dug around, then came up with a small handful of shining gold coins.

"Wow. That makes for terrible accounting, but it's a pretty good work story."

He shoved the gold back in his pocket. "What else can we talk about? TV?"

"Pete, we watch the same TV shows most nights. Sometimes we just start over at the beginning when we get to the end of a series." I groaned and put my head in my hands. "How did we get so boring?"

"Now, come on," he said, "we've done all kinds of things in our time. Remember our sailing days?"

I crossed my arms. I knew I looked sulky, but I couldn't stop myself.

"Remember," he went on, "when you took me to that all night beach bonfire? And then we rolled into the nearest diner and ordered chocolate chip pancakes? With syrup?"

"The carbs!" I let out a laugh. "Holy crap, the things we would eat!"

"And so much pizza," he said, warming to the subject. "We *lived* on pizza some years."

"Now I'm turning into my mother, full of fresh vegetables and fruits and fiber."

"If that's the case, then I'm turning into your mother, too."

"Yeah, but—"

Pete held a finger in the air. His expression turned comically serious. "But nothing. This is our first vacation without the kids. We're going to turn back the clock. We're going to be young and wild and free, even if we have to eat our fruits and vegetables and fiber to do it, and we're going to have *fun*." He emphasized the last word with a thump on the steering wheel.

I punched my fist in the air in solidarity, willing to play along even if I wasn't at all sure of myself. "Fun, dammit!"

2

The Vivacqua Resort lay a few miles south of Sparkle Beach, over a tall bridge across the Intracoastal River. Tiny islands covered in swamp grass and palmettos dotted the river, and seagulls whipped by in chaotic flocks. The winding road led us deep into the peninsula, ending at a large sign with elegant gold lettering spelling out the name of the resort.

Pete drove through the resort gates, eased the SUV over a very high speed bump, and presented our reservation at the security hut.

The gray-haired security guard slowly leaned down to the driver's side window. He peered at us with a mischievous twinkle in his eye. "You two on your honeymoon?"

"Yes, sir," said Pete, with a straight face.

The guard returned the reservation paper with a flourish and a smile. "Valet parking straight ahead, self-parking straight ahead and to the right. You all have fun, now."

"All the fun that's legally possible," Pete replied. He rolled up the window and drove on.

The road twisted through the sprawling grounds of the Vivacqua Resort. Occasionally a gap in the landscaping revealed a peek of the Atlantic Ocean to the east, the Intracoastal Waterway to the west, or the Sparkle Beach lighthouse to the north, across the bay. The hotel itself rose like a giant folded triangle above the landscape.

"Ooh, pretty!" I was already starting to feel better about the trip.

"See? I told you it would be fine," said Pete.

I grabbed his arm. "Pete—let's do valet! We never do valet!"

"Valet the lady wants, valet the lady gets."

He piloted the SUV into the covered hotel driveway.

Baggage handlers weaved through the cars with tall brass rolling carts. Valets jogged by, keys in hand, returning to the valet stand at the side of the hotel entrance. A banner welcoming guests to the Sparkle Beach Regatta hung above.

"Do you remember how much to tip?" I made a face. "Do we tip now or later?"

He drummed his fingers on the wheel. "Um . . ."

I reached for my wallet. "I think I have some ones."

I didn't. I had about a pound of change, but no bills. And Pete made a point of being cash-free at all times, preferring to put everything on a card. The gold coins in his pocket were no help.

A uniformed valet approached.

"They're here," Pete said. He hopped out and went for the luggage in the back.

I counted out a handful of quarters, dimes, and nickels and held them tightly in my fist, then opened the door with the other hand. I intercepted the valet while Pete took the luggage to the curb. "Here." I poured the tip into his hands. "Sorry about the coins!" I scampered away to join Pete.

"Did you tip him?"

"Uh-huh." I smiled innocently at my husband.

He smiled back, totally unaware I'd unloaded half a pound of metal on the poor man.

We proceeded through the glass doors and entered the soaring atrium. Two macaws squawked from perches nestled in the lobby greenery. Fountains splashed softly over stone. Twin elevators slipped up and down the inside of the tower.

I tugged Pete's hand. "Let's make a wish."

We followed an indoor stream to its origin at one of the fountains.

I dug in my pocket for leftover coins and came up with a penny.

"What shall we wish?" said Pete.

I paused, then held up the penny. "Best vacation ever."

"Wait." He rummaged in his pocket and brought out a tiny gold coin. "We should invest a little."

I laughed. "Is this a wish or some kind of weird offering to the vacation gods?"

"Either way, it all goes to charity." Light flashed across the coin as he tilted it this way and that.

I returned the penny to my own pocket. "You're on. Let's do this." I gripped half of the gold coin. Why did the stakes feel so high? Pete had only meant to use the gold coin for fun, and yet I was starting to sweat over the fact that this vacation had to show we still meant something to each other when the kids weren't around. "On the count of three?"

He nodded. "Count us down."

"One, two, three!"

We threw the coin. "Best vacation ever!" we cried.

It landed in the tumbling water.

Pete turned away from the fountain to survey the lobby. "Is that the check-in desk, or the concierge?"

I almost turned away, too—but I noticed a strange movement, as if the waterfall was no longer obeying the law of gravity.

Tendrils of water floated free of the cascade.

And they were heading for *me*.

"Uh-oh," I said.

Pete turned back. "What's uh-oh?"

I spun around, my back to the waterfall. "Nothing. I just forgot to text Luella and Rose this morning. Could you do the check-in thing and I'll send them a quick message?"

You don't get to be married for as long as Pete and me without developing a sixth sense for when your spouse is telling a fib. I could tell Pete's radar was starting to ping—so I grabbed him and gave him a quick kiss right on the lips, hoping the surprise display of affection would throw him off. "Thanks!" I chirped.

He touched his lips. "No problem," he said, with a slightly puzzled look on his face. He wandered off in the direction of the check-in desk.

I whirled around to the waterfall. "Listen, you. Stop trying to blow my cover." I made what I hoped was a subtle pass with my hand. Magical silver sparkles settled over the floating streams of water, and the tendrils dropped obediently back into the waterfall as if they'd never been anywhere else.

I backed away from the water feature to what I guessed was a safe distance. Then I pulled out my phone and called Queenie Russell, my boss at the sunscreen factory, and the only other water witch I knew.

The phone rang and rang.

Queenie was the one who introduced us to all of this in the first place. In addition to being my employer, she'd been my guide and my mentor ever since I'd discovered I had magical powers, right down to taking me out to surf with her to better learn the ways of water magic. If anyone would know what to do, she would.

I hoped.

"Hello?" she answered.

Relief rushed through me. "Queenie!"

"Well, hello, darling, how nice to hear from you—"

"Queenie, listen. Something's going on. I know we can't talk about these things on the phone, but—"

"Pepper, you know the rules," she said. "It'll have to wait for when we see each other in person. How about when you come back to work?"

"No, it can't wait! I'm supposed to be on vacation but things keep happening and I don't know what to do."

"Oh, that's right, you're on vacation! Congratulations, darling, I hope you have a simply *marvelous* time."

"It would be a marvelous time if things didn't keep happening!"

"Haven't you told your husband yet?"

"No, I haven't told him yet! What if he thinks I'm a freak?" I kept my eyes on Pete, who was still at the check-in desk.

"You should tell him," she said, sounding completely unperturbed.

"You're not helping!"

Pete turned from the desk.

I hung up and quickly lowered the phone, with a twinge of guilt for hanging up on Queenie. Hopefully she'd forgive me.

Pete approached, waving a check-in folder with our last name—Monaco—engraved on the top edge. "All set. Room keys, resort map, room service menu. And a complimentary glass of champagne if we want one."

"I'll take that." I needed it.

We received our champagne. I carried the full glasses in my hands and the folder under one arm; Pete managed the luggage. We rode the elevator up to our floor, found our room, and entered.

The curtains had been thrown open, revealing a stunning dual view of the gray-blue Atlantic waves on one side, and the rippling greenish-brown waters of the bay on the other. The red Sparkle Beach lighthouse rose in the distance. From the height of our room, the pool area and minigolf course below looked like children's playsets.

Pete abandoned the luggage and came to the window.

I handed him his glass. "Best vacation ever?"

"Best vacation ever." He struck the glass lightly against mine, then took a small sip and grimaced. "I wish I liked wine."

"I'll have it." I took his glass and set it on the sleek, glass-topped dresser. I drank my own champagne slowly, feeling the bubbles tickle my throat. When the last of it had slipped down, I looked at my husband.

Was this where the romance was supposed to start?

Pete removed his hat, rubbed his hand over his hair, and gave me a bashful grin. He kissed my cheek, as quick and as unexpected as I'd kissed him at the waterfall. "I think I'll take a shower."

Was he feeling as awkward as I was?

The second the bathroom door closed, I took my phone out and composed a text message for my group chat with Luella and Rose: *It keeps getting worse!* I settled on the king bed to await a response. While I waited, I polished off Pete's champagne, too.

Have you talked to Queenie? replied Rose.

Yes, I wrote, *but since we can't discuss it over the phone, she couldn't say anything about it. And I can't drive back to town without Pete noticing I've disappeared.*

Is there anything we can do? asked Luella.

I don't know! What should I do if it keeps happening? I added several grimacing face emojis to get the point across.

If you need us, we'll be there, said Rose.

I've been wanting to check out the Vivacqua for ages, added Luella.

I exhaled. The thought of having backup available brought on a wave of relief. *Okay. Thank you! I don't know if it'll come to that, but if it does I'll let you know.* I set the phone on the hotel nightstand and lay back against the raft of white pillows.

The white noise of the shower, combined with the champagne, lulled my tight muscles into a false sense of relaxation. I could pretend I had no responsibilities, no worries, just for a minute. I snuggled deeper into the crisp sheets and promised myself I wouldn't fall asleep.

3

I woke when the bathroom door opened.

"Pepper?" said Pete, with a weird sort of urgency.

Was he upset I'd conked out? That wouldn't be like him. "I'm not asleep," I said, into the pillow. "I'm just resting my eyes." The champagne made me too fuzzy to think.

"Pepper," he said, with the same urgent tone. "*Look.*"

I slowly rolled onto my back and dragged my heavy eyelids open.

Thousands of round, crystalline water droplets hung in the air like rain in a freeze-frame, catching glints of light from the sun.

I shrieked and sat up, instantly sober.

The droplets fell out of the air all at once with a sound like a machine gun volley.

Pete remained frozen where he stood, a towel wrapped around his waist. He touched the water that had fallen on his shoulders, then stared at the moisture on his fingertips. "What in the world?"

I touched my wet hair and ran my hands over the wet duvet cover. "Condensation from the shower?"

He raised one eyebrow.

"Sprinkler trouble?"

His gaze shifted to the wall-mounted sprinkler, which was one of the only dry things in the room. "I think we should change rooms."

I leaped out of bed. My feet hit the wet, chilly carpet. "No, this is fine! It'll dry." I went to the thermostat and punched the button to drop the temperature several degrees. "See? I'll crank up the air, and it'll be dry in no time."

Pete cocked his head. "Are you . . . *sure* you're okay? You're not acting like yourself. Usually you'd already be on the phone to the front desk."

"I'm learning to be chill," I said.

"You? Chill?"

I approached him and traced my fingertips through the water speckling his bare shoulders. "Don't you like the new 'chill' me?"

He cleared his throat. "Uh, sure . . ."

"Well, then," I said, "why don't we find something to do until the bed is dry, and then . . ." I raised my eyebrows.

"Oh," he said, comprehension dawning. "Right. Yes. Good plan. I'll just"—he gestured over his shoulder, toward the bathroom—"get dressed." He retreated and shut the door.

I kicked the bed. "Stupid magic. Can't even take a nap!" I put my hands on my hips. Why did these things keep happening? What was I going to do?

I grabbed my phone from the nightstand. *Change of plans*, I wrote. *I need you. It's getting worse.*

How about tomorrow morning? Luella replied.

I paused to think about it. Pete loved to sleep in when he got the chance, and he wouldn't think it was unusual if I got up earlier to go for a walk or a swim. *Yes, that works*, I said. *Is that okay for you, Rose?*

I'll be there, she said.

I gave them directions and made a note to call security to make sure my friends were added to the visitor list.

The bathroom door clicked open.

I hastily stuffed the phone in my purse.

Pete emerged. "You hungry? We could have dinner at the all-day brunch at the restaurant downstairs. Chocolate chip pancakes, for old times' sake?"

I hooked my arm through his. "You read my mind."

We rode the elevator down to the restaurant. Across the dining room, an elaborate fountain rose all the way to the second-floor ceiling. Water spilled from beneath a life-size bronze mermaid at the top of the fountain, then cascaded through oversized stone oyster shells, and danced around smaller bronze children sculpted to look like aquatic cherubs. The sun bathed everything with golden light.

The uniformed hostess picked up two menus from the stack on the podium. "Welcome to Cascades. Party of two?"

We nodded.

"Follow me." She led the way through the restaurant to a table adjacent to the fountain. "Your server will be here in a moment."

We sat and picked up the menus.

"That's quite a fountain," said Pete.

I eyed the water with suspicion. Hopefully it wouldn't decide to leap out and drench us at any moment. "What are you having?"

"Chocolate chip pancakes and bacon. You only live once." He set the menu neatly to the side. "You?"

"Same, but with sausage." I scanned the menu. "Oh, look! They have fresh-squeezed orange juice. Hmm . . . glass or carafe?"

"The eternal question," said Pete. "Get the carafe, I'll split it with you."

We ordered our carbohydrate fiesta.

Pete fiddled with his water glass.

I gave it a look, silently willing it to not do anything noticeable. "So . . . movies? Politics?"

"Let's go with movies." He took a sip of water. "I saw a good one on the classic movie channel one night a few weeks ago, when I couldn't sleep."

"Oh, yeah?" I drank from my own glass. "What was it?"

"*Bell, Book, and Candle.*"

I choked on my water and coughed uncontrollably. He made as if to get up, but I waved him back. "I'm fine." It came out strangled. I cleared my throat.

When he was satisfied that I wasn't going to expire right there at the table, he continued. "You know the one, right? The fifties movie, with Kim Novak and Jimmy Stewart? The witch puts a spell on her neighbor so he won't marry her awful old college chum—but she ends up falling for him and losing her powers."

"How romantic," I said, resisting the urge to stick out my tongue in disgust.

The waiter delivered the carafe of orange juice and two glasses.

I poured. "I mean—really? What a stupid tradeoff. Why can't she fall in love and keep her powers? What kind of garbage is that?" Pete opened his mouth like he might have said something, but I kept going. "It's old-fashioned sexism, that's what it is. 1950s nonsense. Like a woman can't be powerful and romantic at the same time." I made a disbelieving noise. "If you were the Jimmy Stewart character, wouldn't you think it would be cool to have a witch for a wife?"

Pete gazed out the window, either tracking a bird in flight, or not taking the conversation seriously, or avoiding conflict.

Or all of the above.

I leaned in. "Back then they were just threatened by the thought of a woman having more power than a man. And you wouldn't be threatened by that, would you?" I casually tossed my hair.

"Hmm?" His benign gaze returned to me. "Of course not."

Did he mean it?

I didn't follow up because our pancakes arrived. We dug in, and for a few minutes, the only sounds were the splashing fountain, the hum of other conversations, and the clink of silverware and glasses.

When we finished, we both leaned back from the table with audible sighs. I rubbed my belly; he patted his. Our gazes met, and we both chuckled.

"You think the room is dry yet?" he asked.

"Almost. I could use a little time to digest. How about a walk?"

Pete signaled for the check.

We left Cascades and went to the elevated garden walkway outside. One stretch of the boardwalk wound over the sea oats and down a flight of stairs to the beach itself; another ran around the hotel to the marina, the bay, and the surrounding wetlands.

I chose the ocean path. The sea breeze tossed my curls and fluttered Pete's shirt as we went down the stairs to the sand. Waves crashed in the shallows, sending up bits of foam. Sandpipers scurried to and fro around the waves.

My husband reached for his back pocket. "Do you think we should check on the kids?"

I slapped his hand away. "You're worse than I am. We haven't been gone for more than a few hours, and we're hardly any farther away than when we go to work."

"I know, but—"

"But me no buts. If I have to be strong, you have to be strong." I splashed him with my foot.

He danced back, then pointed a finger at me. "Of course, you know this means war." He charged me and kicked a wave in my direction.

I laughed and ran into deeper water. "Oh, yeah? Come and get me!"

He stalked closer.

I crouched, ready to dart in either direction.

Suddenly, he stopped. His gaze focused over my shoulder, and his eyes widened. "Look out!"

I turned.

A six-foot wave barreled toward me out of absolutely nowhere. I had scarcely a second to react—I threw my arms up.

The wave smashed in two, splitting itself just in time as it crashed past me.

As it ebbed, I turned to look for Pete.

He slogged through the knee-deep water. "How did that wave miss you? It was coming right at you. I thought it was going to knock you down."

"I don't know." My voice shook. I'd used my magic to blast the wave apart, right in front of him—and I'd *never* used my magic in front of him before. "I got lucky, I guess."

We walked back to the dry, fluffy sand, away from the surf, then up the stairs to the boardwalk. I turned and leaned on the railing for one last view of the churning water before we returned to the resort grounds.

We were staring across the waves, breathing the salty air in silence, when suddenly a long, skinny brown animal scampered out of the bobbing sea oats and hopped across the beach. It ran with a sinuous motion, trailing a long, sleek tail behind it. Its fur glistened with moisture.

"What's a river otter doing on the beach?" I said.

Pete blinked. "What river otter?"

I took my gaze off the otter to stare at Pete. "What do you mean?"

"I mean I don't see an otter." He scanned the beach.

I looked back.

It was gone.

4

By the time we returned to the fountain-filled lobby, even the squawking parrots seemed to echo my anxiety. I'd lost it. I'd fired off magic without a thought for the consequences—and then I saw an otter that may or may not have actually existed.

I needed a reset.

"You know what?" I said to Pete as we approached the elevators. "I'd like to take a hot bath."

"Absolutely. No problem." He checked his watch. "I think I'll explore a bit. Join you in, say, an hour?"

Was he delaying, too? I put on a smile to cover the uneasiness that had just ratcheted up another notch. "An hour sounds good."

I stepped into the elevator. He waved as the doors closed between us.

The elevator surged upward fast enough to make my stomach drop. I watched the floor numbers climb higher until the elevator stopped and the doors slid open.

I entered the room alone, took a complimentary bathrobe from the closet, and slipped into the bathroom. A quick shower to wash up—then a long soak in the extra-deep tub. We would start our vacation over again, minus the weird water, the disappearing otter, and whatever awkwardness was between us. I sank into the steaming water with a sigh and laid the hot washcloth over my eyes.

Why couldn't I just tell Pete about my magic? Why was it never the right time? Was it a complication so big I didn't trust bringing it into our lives? It was complicated enough to raise two kids with both of us working and being busy every minute of every day.

So what if a little water had started splashing around uncontrollably—I could make an excuse, and my friends could surely help me get it under control again. No need to bother Pete with it.

When the water had cooled, I pushed the lever to drain the tub, then stepped out to grab the bathrobe. I slipped it on and tied the belt.

The tub faucet gurgled out a stream of water.

Weird. You'd think a fancy hotel would have its plumbing in good working order. I pushed the handle firmly to the off position.

The water didn't stop. Instead, it sprayed out like a backyard hose, rapidly filling the tub back up—and the water wasn't going down the drain.

I knelt by the tub and fiddled with the lever.

Nothing happened, other than the tub continuing to fill.

Panic rose like the water. I swept my fingers over the drain in case I'd clogged it somehow, with stray hairs or a clump of soap.

All at once, the water stopped shooting out of the faucet. I rocked back on my heels with relief. At least the tub wouldn't overflow.

Then—the water rose from the tub like a floating ice sculpture.

My mouth fell open.

This couldn't be good.

The water formed an amorphous blob. It stretched upward.

I stood and staggered back, scrabbling to bring something defensive to hand without taking my eyes off the thing, but I only came up with a handful of washcloths.

The water took on the shape of a thick cylinder, roughly the diameter of a tree trunk, reaching to a height of about six feet. It extended what looked like a branch—then another branch—and finally the base of it split into two.

Not branches—arms and legs! Was it a water monster? I took my eyes off it in a desperate bid to find *something* to defend myself with.

A soap dish, a water glass, and an unplugged hair dryer. Not the best options. I grabbed the hairdryer and held it like a gun.

Whatever this thing was, I couldn't just run away. If it had to do with water, it had to do with me. Better to face it now, before Pete came back; before he caught me in a battle with a tubful of rogue enchanted water.

A head formed on the watery shape. The torso chiseled and narrowed itself to a recognizable waist. A hand and fingers formed at the end of each liquid arm. Then, in a blink, the whole thing went from transparent liquid to something quite solid.

A muscular young man stood before me, his hair wet and wavy underneath a braided garland of green leaves. He had a water lily threaded into the green leafy crown, and stone bracelets on each wrist. He looked to be about twenty-five.

And . . . he was naked. Very naked.

I should have screamed, but only a faint squeak came out.

He bowed from the waist and stayed that way. "Greetings, lady. Do I have the honor of addressing the youngest witch?"

I blinked. The youngest witch? Me? I aimed the hairdryer like a TV cop. The cord dangled. "Freeze," I said, with all the authority I could muster.

He started to raise his head, but appeared to think better of it, and stayed in his uncomfortable-looking position. "If it pleases my lady."

With my free hand, I snatched a bath towel from the nearest rack and held it under the intruder's nose until he took it. "Here. Put this on, and you can stop bowing."

He swung the towel over his shoulders and straightened up.

I closed my eyes and squeezed the bridge of my nose. Surely he wasn't that dense. "That's not where the towel goes."

A rustle of the towel being moved. "How about this?"

I opened my eyes.

He'd put it over his head like he was the Virgin Mary, and he was smiling like an idiot.

"Oh, for God's sake." I clearly wasn't in any danger from this dude, whoever he was. I dropped the hairdryer on the counter, tugged my own bathrobe tighter, and re-secured the ties so I could move freely. Then I snatched the towel off his head and held it like a rectangular shield between us. "Put it around your waist."

He took the towel solemnly, with smooth, unlined hands, and wrapped it clumsily around himself. "My apologies, lady witch. I am not accustomed to these coverings."

"Don't call me that! And how do you even know I'm a witch?" I glanced anxiously at the bathroom door. I'd soaked in the bath for ages. Pete would be back any minute. "Never mind. Whoever you are, you need to leave. Right now."

The electronic lock clicked loudly and the hotel room door made a racket as it opened.

"I'm back!" my husband called. "Did you have a nice bath?"

Several whispered curse words left my lips, words I never, *ever* used around the kids. "You!" I whispered to the bathwater man. "Get lost!"

His eyes widened. "I cannot! Once I take this form, I must return home before I can change again!"

I stifled a scream by bringing my wrists to my face and biting the bunched sleeves of my robe.

Pete knocked lightly on the bathroom door. "You all right in there?"

"I'm fine," I called.

How could this possibly be happening to me? How was I going to explain a nude man hanging out in the bathroom?

"Are you visible to other people?" I whispered. "*Normal* people, I mean?"

"Yes—I am sorry!" He clasped his hands in an apologetic gesture. The towel, which he'd been holding up, crumpled into the floor of the tub, leaving him one-hundred-percent naked.

Again.

I squeezed my eyes shut and reopened them. "Don't say a word. Don't even breathe, do you understand?"

He nodded.

"And pick up your towel!" I snatched the curtain closed.

I turned to the mirror. My curls look like I'd run through a thunderstorm, complete with lightning strike. What was I going to do? There was no other place to hide the strange young man. Pete was waiting for me to emerge. We'd both been clear about our romantic intentions for the evening.

I'd have to make an excuse to get Pete out of the room again.

I straightened my bathrobe, squared my shoulders, and walked out of the bathroom, shutting the door behind me.

Pete was lying on the bed, his arms propped behind his head. "Well, hello, stranger."

I laughed in what I hoped was a coquettish fashion—but not *too* coquettish, because I needed to get the naked man out of our room before anything got too frisky. "Hello there."

He hopped up. "I think I'll use the bathroom myself."

Oh, crap. I hadn't thought of that.

Pete caught what must have been a very alarmed look on my face. "Don't worry," he said as he strode past. "I won't be long."

When the bathroom door closed, I dropped to my knees next to the bed and cradled my face in my hands. Every noise felt like a nail in a coffin: the toilet lid, up; the toilet seat, down; the flush; the water in the sink.

He was almost out. I dared to breathe. I was going to get away with it. It was going to be fine.

Then—

The sound of the shower curtain sliding along the rail. Then silence.

"Please, please, don't let this happen to me," I said to whatever powers might be listening. "I'm not ready to to tell him—"

"Pepper?" he called. "Pepper, there's a man in here." Another pause. "He seems to be bowing to me."

I slumped.

Pete continued, almost too calmly. "He also appears to be entirely without clothing."

I dragged myself to my feet. The jig was up.

"Any thoughts, Pep?"

I crossed the room in what felt like slow motion. I entered the bathroom. Sure enough, the visitor was bowing in that uncomfortable-looking position again.

When he saw me, he straightened, revealing his statu-esque body in its full glory.

He hadn't picked up the towel.

Pete's eyebrows flew up.

"Lady witch," the young man said, "I fear I have not made this fine gentleman's acquaintance."

"Lady *what*?" said Pete.

Whatever I had planned to say evaporated. Staring at the strange naked man, along with my husband, in the close quarters of a hotel bathroom, demolished anything that could have passed for an explanation or excuse. "Pete, do you think you could lend him a pair of shorts?"

"Shorts?" Pete echoed.

"I would be honored to have your shorts," said the stranger, with a smaller bow.

Pete's eyes were taking on the glazed look of incipient shock. He didn't move, other than to put out a hand to the counter for support.

"I'll get them!" I ran out and quickly unzipped Pete's suitcase. I pulled out his swim trunks, which had an elastic waistband, and would be the most likely thing to fit. I hurried back to the bathroom. "Here." I handed the shorts to the stranger.

"I am most grateful." He began to sling the shorts around his shoulders, but he caught my desperate headshake. He slowly lowered them to waist level, then smiled.

Pete was as still as if he'd been carved from salt.

I cleared my throat. "You have to actually put them on your legs." I mimed stepping into pants.

"Ah." He lifted his leg theatrically. "Like so."

"Not yet!" I said to the intruder. I tugged at Pete. "Come on. Let's give him some privacy."

"Privacy," echoed Pete. He stumbled out of the bathroom under my guidance.

I shut the door.

"Pepper," he said. "There's a naked man in our room."

"There, there," I said, patting his arm. "He's putting on shorts right now."

"Pepper," he said, "he called you a witch."

"I know, my love."

A loud thump came from within the bathroom.

"It is well!" called the stranger. "I but lost my footing. I have recovered now." The door rattled, like someone was wrestling with the doorknob, then opened. In shorts, the stranger looked like a normal, well-formed twentysomething, although the green garland, the water lily, and the bracelets gave him a hippie surfer vibe.

"Why don't we all sit down and have a nice chat?" I gestured toward the small table by the window, with two chairs and an adjacent lounge.

Pete swayed, but didn't move.

I steered him to the closest chair and gave him a gentle push until he dropped into it.

The stranger remained standing. He tugged at the swim trunks. "This is passing strange indeed, but I must say, it is an honor to introduce myself to you, lady witch. And your boon companion." He aimed a courteous nod in Pete's direction.

Pete's eyes regained a more focused look, and he trained his gaze on the man who'd borrowed his trunks. "There's that witch thing again." He paused and glanced at me. "Does that make me a boon companion? Or am I playing the Jimmy Stewart character?"

I laid a hand on his shoulder to hush him. "Tell us who you are."

The stranger stood straight. "My name is unspeakable. No. Your pardons, please. I am starting all wrong. My name is *unpronounceable* to humans." He smiled, seemingly with relief for getting the explanation right. "I am lately of the mixed waters of yonder bay, and the fresh waters beyond that, belonging to the Sweetwater Folk."

"Unpronounceable name, mixed waters, fresh waters, Sweetwater Folk. Got it." I didn't get it at all. I had no idea what he was talking about. "But what are you here for?"

"Did I not say? Your pardon, lady witch." He laid a hand on his chest. "I come to beg a favor."

5

Pete raised a single finger. "Hold on a moment." He rotated his finger backward. "Rewind. Why do you keep calling my wife a witch?"

"No offense intended, good sir." The stranger made a brief bow in Pete's direction, then spoke with slow, careful enunciation, as if speaking to someone hard of hearing. "Because she is a witch."

Pete let out a forced-sounding chuckle. "Very funny." He steepled his fingers. "Where are the hidden cameras?"

This was it. No more hiding. Suddenly, my feet became the most interesting thing in the world to look at. "Pete . . . I *am* a witch."

"Don't be silly. There's no such thing," he replied, with the calm air of someone saying *the sky is cloudy*, or *the earth is round.*

My head snapped up. "There certainly is."

"Oh, are we living the remake of *Bell, Book, and Candle?*"

"Well, you're already married to me and I haven't lost my powers yet, so no."

He gave me a skeptical look over the rims of his glasses.

"You don't believe me? Fine, I'll show you." I stood, took a glass from the dresser, and went to the bathroom sink. I filled the glass with water, carried it back to the table, and set it down. "Watch." I stared at the water until it rose under my power to float in the air like a tiny balloon surrounded with silver sparks. I made a twisting and pulling motion to straighten it out as if it were a long strand of pasta. I sent the stream of water toward Pete's head.

He pressed back against his chair, too stunned to even dodge.

A flick of my fingers shifted the water's path. The stream took a turn, floating around his head, then rising to encircle it like a halo.

Pete carefully tilted his head to watch the water halo rotate.

I guided the water back into the glass without spilling a drop, then put my hands on my hips and shot my husband a challenging stare.

"That's . . . quite the feat." As calm as he appeared, his voice wobbled. He leaned toward me. "Why didn't you tell me? And how long have you known?"

Although the stranger didn't have the slightest idea what to do with a pair of shorts, he did have the grace to look away and pretend not to listen.

"Since last summer," I said. "I'm sorry! I was afraid you'd think I was crazy. Or a freak. Or that you wouldn't want to be married to someone with magical powers. That you'd think I was dangerous or something."

"Are you?"

"Of course not!"

"I mean, you've always been a little wild," said Pete. "Look how you ate that whole stack of chocolate chip pancakes." He glanced at the stranger, who was studiously staring at the ceiling. "Did your magic powers make this guy show up? Also, we can't keep referring to him without a name."

At least the conversation had veered away from me. "Hey, you," I said to the young man wearing Pete's shorts.

He snapped to attention.

"My husband's right. Is there something pronounceable we can call you?"

He blinked. Obviously, this was not something that had occurred to him.

"What do you like to do?" asked Pete. "Maybe there's something we can use for a name."

"Well," said the stranger, with an air of wanting to please, "I like to swim and fish."

"There you have it." Pete made a motion like casting a lure. "He's a fisher."

I nodded. "Fisher's a good name."

"I accept your kind gift," said the newly-named stranger. "A Fisher I shall be."

"And I'm Pepper, and this is Pete." I dusted my hands. "Now that's settled, let's talk." I remembered Queenie running the witches' meeting at Suntan Queen, and did my best to take on her aura of authority—even though I had absolutely no idea what to do next. "Who are you? For that matter, *what* are you? I've never seen any magic that turns a person into water."

"The water form is one of three. The other two are what you see before you, and the fish-tailed form."

"You're a mermaid? I mean—a mer*man*?"

Fisher nodded.

"Or is 'merpeople' the proper term?" said Pete.

I elbowed him. "And you call yourselves the Sweetwater Folk? Why 'Sweetwater'?"

"Our territory consists of the rivers and springs. Sweet water."

"What about the ocean?"

Fisher's face took on a troubled look. "The ocean belongs to the Saltwater Folk."

"The ocean merpeople," I said. "Are they bad?"

Fisher shook his head. "No, not at all. I have misspoken again—I apologize. I believe the dryness distracts me." He looked at us hopefully. "Perchance we may continue our conversation in your water cave?"

"Water cave?"

"He means the bathroom," said Pete.

"Oh. As long as you keep your pants on," I said.

"A thousand thanks!" He padded away into the bathroom.

"You're sure you're not mad?" I asked Pete. "I really was hoping he'd go away and leave us alone. So we'd have some, uh"—I cleared my throat—"time to ourselves."

Pete chuckled. "Best vacation ever."

"You're sure?"

He stood, then leaned down to my ear. "Actually, I'm kind of digging the idea of a powerful witchy wife."

I felt a blush creep over my cheeks.

Fisher's voice came from the bathroom: "What strange magic is this?"

"Let's go before he breaks something we have to pay for," I said.

We entered the bathroom. Fisher had his hands wrapped around the showerhead in what looked like an attempt to unscrew it.

"Not like that," said Pete, removing Fisher's grip and re-tightening the showerhead. "Like so." He turned on the water.

"And if I should wish for it not to drain?"

Pete flipped the lever.

Fisher beamed under the blast of water. It pooled around his feet and filled the air with cool mist.

I smiled back. "Almost like home, huh?"

"My gratitude is boundless! A thousand favors I will owe you before this day is through."

"Speaking of favors," I said to the showering merman, "what is this favor you want me to do?"

The water ran over Fisher's face. "I am charged to bring you to the court of the Sweetwater Folk."

"That's the favor? To go to your court?"

"Not so, lady witch. To bring you to the court is my charge; the favor will be asked of you there."

"Can't you just tell me what it is?"

"I cannot. The queen would have my very tail for it."

My eyebrows rose. "So you have a queen?"

"Do you not have a queen?" asked Fisher, shuffling around in the water that had risen to his ankles.

"Nope," I said. "But my boss is named Queenie."

"Passing strange," said Fisher, "to have no queen."

"Why ask *me* for a favor, though?"

"Did I not say?" He turned to let the water hit his broad back. "Because you are the youngest witch near our waters. We have a saying: 'When the young dispute, the aged resolve; when the aged dispute, the young resolve.'"

I snorted. "I think you have the wrong witch. I'm in my forties."

Fisher shook his head. "Lady witch, in your years, our queen is well beyond her fifth century."

6

A half-millenium-old mermaid queen lived in Sparkle Beach? "Pardon us," I said to Fisher. I pulled a reluctant Pete out of the bathroom to the relative privacy of the bedroom. I sat heavily on the edge of the bed. "This is insane."

Pete paced the floor, looking as happy as a middle-aged man with a new motorcycle.

"Are you hearing me at all, Peter?"

He stopped. "Of course I am."

I sprang up. "Then you see how insane this is. I'm not some twentysomething; I can't go running off after some quest from some merman I don't even know!"

"Oh, come now," said Pete. "He seems perfectly respectable."

"Exactly! No one acts like that unless they're up to something."

"I think he seems like a very nice young merman."

I threw up my hands.

"Pepper, Pepper." He came up behind me, smoothed his hands over my shoulders, and massaged the knots. "You're doubting yourself."

I whirled on him. "I'm not doubting myself!"

"Then why would you turn down the opportunity for adventure?"

My mouth opened and closed.

"You said it yourself: 'We're boring.' Now you have the chance to do something that's the complete *opposite* of boring. What does being twenty, thirty, forty, or eighty have to do with it?"

"I—"

"Tell me a real reason why you shouldn't see this through."

My voice softened. "What if it's dangerous?"

"Do you think that's a concern?"

"The boys . . . what if something happened to me?"

"Do you remember when Rocky was born?"

I blinked. "What?"

"Do you remember when Rocky was born?" he repeated.

I gave him a look. "Have you lost your mind? Of course I do."

"Remember how scared we were? We had never had a child before; we had no idea what we were doing."

"Yeah, and that hospital lactation consultant wouldn't give me a freaking nipple shield when I asked for one."

He clapped his hands together. "That's my point. You already had good instincts of what to do. You just needed to be able to follow them."

"What are you saying? That following Fisher to the mer-people court is like asking for a nipple shield?"

"What I'm saying, you obstinate minx, is that you should trust your instincts." He tugged lightly on one of my curls. "If you're worried about danger . . . do you have any witch friends who could help out?"

Hope started to bubble like a spring. "But what about our vacation?"

"The resort will still be here."

"But my parents are watching the kids . . ."

"Perfect timing."

I paced the floor. Who was I? A wife? A mother? An accountant? A witch? And if I was the "fun" one, why did the idea of doing something *because I wanted to do it* make me feel like a tiny Fred Astaire was tap-dancing through my stomach?

No matter how much I played at being the life of the party, the truth was: I became an accountant and married a dentist. I took the safe path—and it worked, too. What a nice house we had, with a pool and all.

And yet . . .

I wanted more than just a slow slide to old age where I would look back and say, "Well, that was nice." *Nice* was fine. But I wanted it all. I wanted *adventure*.

And no one was going to stop me.

Not even me.

"Get Fisher," I said.

"That's my girl," said Pete.

When Fisher came out, he didn't bother to dry off. He gave a short bow; water dripped from his limbs. "You summoned me, lady witch?"

"I will go with you."

He lit up, and opened his mouth to speak.

"But"—I held up a hand—"I need to talk to my friends."

Fisher tilted his head like a confused puppy. "Friends?"

"Witch friends." Again he opened his mouth to speak, but I cut him off. "And I need some time. I assume this 'court' is somewhere off the beaten path?"

Fisher nodded.

"Right. I'll need to get ready, too. It's not like we can leave right now." I looked at Pete. "Where on earth are we going to put him until then?"

"I shall stay by your side, lady," said Fisher.

Pete pushed his glasses up. "This may be a king-sized bed, Fisher, but I'm not making room for a third."

"Hang on, let me think." I snapped my fingers. "I know exactly where Fisher would feel at home. We'll need to drive him there, though."

"We really ought to get him a shirt," said Pete.

We drove out of the resort with Fisher curiously examining his new tie-dyed "I Went to Sparkle Beach and All I Got Was This T-Shirt" top, along with the seatbelt, the cupholder, the windows, and anything else within reach.

Pete turned to the backseat. "Fisher, don't unbuckle." He turned back around. "It's like having a toddler all over again."

"Remember how Rocky used to scale the side of the crib and escape?"

"And Kevin used to run away whenever we took him to a store. Those were the days."

Fisher leaned forward. "Are these your heirs?"

I laughed. "Heirs? I guess you could call them that. Oops—I think we broke a rule."

"What are these 'rules'?" asked Fisher.

"When we go out together, we're not supposed to discuss kids, work, or stress," said Pete.

"You are wise," said Fisher. He pressed his nose to the window. "Are we there yet?"

"Not quite," I said, hanging a right to head for Sparkle Beach proper. We passed Highway to Grill and crossed the Intracoastal Waterway bridge. Immediately after the bridge, I took the riverside road north along the peninsula.

A few minutes later, we pulled up to a house with tall windows and flat sections of roof at different heights. The house was partially hidden by thick tropical landscaping.

"This is it," I said.

"This is your boss's house," said Pete. "I recognize the convertible."

"Yup."

"Why would you bring a merman to your boss's house?"

"Surprise—she's a witch." I didn't pause for his reaction. If he was going to come along, he was going to have to keep up. I turned back to Fisher, who was struggling with the seatbelt. "Push the red thing."

The seatbelt clicked and retracted. He sighed in relief and stretched.

I unbuckled myself and got out while Pete helped Fisher out the passenger door. "She told me she'd be around back."

We walked down a stepping stone garden path that led to the rear of the house. Brightly striped lounge chairs surrounded a kidney-shaped pool overlooking the river. "Queenie?"

"Darlings!" Queenie swept up from her lounge chair with her arms wide open. Her yellow caftan billowed in the breeze. She whipped off her sunglasses and peered at Pete from beneath her wide-brimmed hat. "So you told him." She extended her hand like royalty. Gemstones winked in the sunlight.

Pete took her hand and attempted a good imitation of Fisher's bow. "Yes, my wife told me you're a . . ." He paused, seeming to not want to offend.

"A witch, darling." She turned to the merman.

"And this is—well, we're calling him Fisher, because his true name is too hard to pronounce," I said.

Fisher let out a startling series of squeaks, chirps, and grunts. He gave a bashful smile.

Queenie's finely-plucked eyebrows rose. "Quite. And what are you, Fisher? Are you a witch?"

"I am of the Sweetwater Folk."

She blinked politely.

"What he means to say," I added, "is that he's a merman who can also take human or water form, and he lives in freshwater, and I need you to keep an eye on him for a day or so while I get ready to visit his people. Fisher, Queenie is a water witch like me."

Fisher bowed deeply and stayed low. "I am most honored, lady witch."

Queenie touched his shoulder. "You don't have to stand on ceremony with me, darling." She dropped her hand— then she reached out for one more shoulder squeeze. "My goodness, you're quite muscular, aren't you?"

"I am thought to be so." With an air of willingness to please, Fisher began to pull off his shirt.

"Keep your clothes on," I said.

He dropped the hem. "Yes, lady."

"I don't mind," said Queenie. "Well-formed young men add a certain *je ne sais quoi* to the place."

Pete cleared his throat roughly, as if covering a laugh.

"What do I do if I am dry?" asked Fisher.

"I have the remedy for that, young man," said Queenie. "Have you ever heard of a mai tai?

"Can you swim in it?"

She winked at him. "You certainly can."

"Queenie," I said, "don't get the merman drunk."

Queenie lifted her chin. "Need I remind you who the senior witch is here? Come, Fisher, let us repair to the bar." She laced her arm through his.

"He likes to stay wet," I called, as they walked away.

Queenie waved without turning around.

I watched them go. "You think he'll be all right?"

"Other than that she looked like she wanted to eat him for a snack, I'm sure he'll be fine," said Pete.

7

I woke the next morning to Pete having a quiet conversation at the hotel room door. The door clicked shut, and the smell of bacon, eggs, and fried potatoes reached me where I lay buried under a heap of covers. The sun was rising over the Atlantic Ocean.

Pete carefully carried a tray over and set it on the table by the window. "You're awake—just in time for breakfast." He fiddled with a single pink rose in a bud vase.

I sat up and rubbed my eyes. "Did I dream that a naked man crashed our hotel room?"

"If you did, then we had the exact same dream." He poured two mugs of coffee.

I yawned and took a cup. "Luella and Rose will be here soon." On the way back from Queenie's, I'd already told him about my witchy friends and how they'd be coming to visit in the morning.

"Do you need me, or can I stay here and luxuriate in doing absolutely nothing?"

"Luxuriate."

"Hot damn."

After I ate, showered, and dressed, my phone buzzed. "They're here. I'm heading down."

Pete, still in a fluffy, too-short bathrobe, raised his mug to me over his copy of the Sparkle Beach Journal.

Luella and Rose were wandering the lobby. I couldn't suppress a brief flash of envy. They had the freedom to do whatever they wanted, including rolling up to my hotel on short notice; Luella was already an empty-nester, and Rose seemed unlikely to ever be tied down by anything. Or maybe what I was feeling was gratitude, that they dropped whatever they were doing to help me out.

Call it gratitude with a sprinkle of envy, like a bowl of pea soup with crispy bacon bits on top. "What's up, witches?"

"This place is amazing!" said Luella. She carried a large raffia tote, and wore a colorful tasselled coverup along with flip-flops.

Rose wore a loose black shift and a pair of dark sunglasses. "Where's the pool?"

"This way." I led them down the stairs to the pool area.

Large artificial rock formations surrounded and overhung the pool, creating natural-looking waterfalls and swimmable caves. Palm trees circled the pool deck and offered some shade from the Florida sun.

Rose tilted her sunglasses down. "*Very* nice. Remind me to tell Oliver he's bringing me here."

Lucky for us, it was so early in the morning that we practically had the whole pool to ourselves. We set our things on a nearby table, pulled off our coverups, and waded into the water.

"Ah," sighed Luella. "This is the life."

Rose slowly moved her arms through the water. "So tell us what's going on."

I recapped the previous day, from the strange happenings at home all the way until I dropped off Fisher at Queenie's riverside estate.

Rose swirled the water thoughtfully. "Had Queenie ever heard of these people? The—" She paused, looking for the word.

"Sweetwater and Saltwater Folk? No. Fisher said the queen was over five hundred years old, and he doesn't seem to be very familiar with modern stuff, so I'm guessing they've been underground for a while."

"Possibly literally," said Rose.

"What do you mean?"

"Florida's freshwater is largely underground. There's a whole underground river system."

"Underground merpeople," said Luella, with wide eyes.

We floated into a cave. Light refracted through the water and skittered across the rocky gray walls around us.

"If Queenie didn't know about it, then neither did Hilda—or your mom," Rose said to Luella. "They would have mentioned it at some point."

"Maybe no one knows about them," I said. "He had a funny way of speaking, too. It sure sounded like he didn't get out much. Although he must have learned English some-where. Maybe back in the old days or something."

"What are you going to do?" said Luella.

"I'm going to visit the merpeople. What other option is there?" I sounded more confident and carefree than I felt.

"You could *not* go," Rose said.

Luella splashed her. "And miss the adventure of a lifetime?"

Rose aimed a splash at her in return. "I'm just playing devil's advocate."

Our feet looked blue and wavy beneath the water. "You could come with me."

They regarded me in solemn silence—then burst into laughter.

"You idiot," said Rose. "Of course we're coming with you."

"Wouldn't miss it," added Luella.

They simultaneously splashed me.

I danced backward in the water. "Splash a water witch, will you?" I plunged my hands beneath the surface and used my magic to send a sparkling two-foot wave in their direction.

It hit them head-on.

"Pepper, you witch!" cried Luella. "I actually blew dry my hair this morning!"

I had to dance back again as Luella aimed another splash my way. "Truce! Hold still; I'll dry your hair." I summoned the water from their hair. It lifted free in droplets, then collected into a ball, which I dropped into the pool. "There. Mostly dry."

Luella gingerly touched her hair. "Thank you."

Something moved in my peripheral vision. A shiny brown head poked out from a nook, twitched its whiskers at me, then disappeared. "Hey—the otter!"

Rose looked around. "What otter?"

I slogged through the chest-high water to reach a pool ladder. "That otter!"

"They keep otters in the swimming pool?" asked Luella.

"Come on!" I hauled myself up and out, shedding water in sheets. "No time to waste!"

We dripped our way along the cave pool walkway. The slick floor led to a bridge over the narrow portion of the cave pool. The path on the other side of the bridge led us back into the sunlight next to the open-air part of the pool.

I shaded my eyes. "Where'd it go?"

"There!" cried Luella. She pointed beyond the pool, to the fanciful minigolf course with an oversized fake sand castle decorated with colorful pennants.

We crashed through the bushes and hustled across the course, attracting stares as we went.

"Fore!" I shouted.

"I'm not sure that's the right word for what we're doing," said Rose.

"Who cares?" I said, dodging a surfboard prop and nearly tripping over a fake fish popping out of a blue-carpeted river. The nearest golfer gave us a funny look.

We lost the otter's trail at the ninth hole, which was decorated with giant oyster shells.

"Look—they open and close," said Luella.

The farthest shell creaked open—and the otter popped out and ran for it.

"Go, go, go!" I said.

We rushed after it.

The otter dodged and danced through the bushes, then broke out onto the fourteenth hole, where she leaped onto a slowly rotating miniature Ferris wheel.

Her beady eyes shone as the wheel rotated around. She alternated chirping at us and flexing her curved whiskers.

"Well, I'll be," said Luella.

"Notice anything strange?" Rose said.

We both looked at her.

"No one else has noticed an otter riding a Ferris wheel."

I covered my mouth to stop a cry of triumph. "Don't scare her," I said, in a hushed voice—mostly to myself, since I was the only one talking.

It couldn't be.

But maybe it was.

I carefully crept forward.

"Pepper—" said Luella.

"I got this," I said. I lowered myself to sit criss-cross at the bottom of the Ferris wheel.

The Ferris wheel rotation took the joy-riding otter all the way to the top.

I sat as still as the fake fish statues in the blue carpet pond.

The otter descended—closer, closer—and then she leaped from the basket. She romped around me in a circle, pausing to chase her tail or just roll around on the ground.

I dared to extend my hands.

She paused her play and made a curious squeaking sound. Then she scrambled over my legs, half-climbed my arm, and peered into my face. Her silver whiskers and claws caught the light of the morning sun.

I petted her sleek head and a surge of pure satisfaction filled my heart.

I had found my familiar.

8

"I hate to interrupt," said Rose, "but if you keep petting thin air, people are going to notice."

"Spoilsport," I said, letting the otter climb up to my shoulders and nibble curiously at the decorative metallic buckle on my bathing suit strap.

"She's right," said Luella. "We're already attracting a bit too much attention for crashing the minigolf course in bathing suits."

I looked over my shoulder. Sure enough, the security guard from the day before was a few holes back and gaining on us. "Time to go!"

The otter leaped down.

Luella and Rose helped me up. We hurried out past the eighteenth hole—the one with leaping dolphin statues around a water hazard—and dove around a corner. The otter skidded after us.

I peeked around the rocky outcropping. "I think we lost him."

We tried to look casual as we walked back to the cave—as casual as we could look as a rambunctious otter danced between our feet.

"Will you call it Rocky, or Kevin?" said Rose.

Luella laughed.

Since they were on either side of me, it was easy to punch them both in the arm simultaneously. "Shut up. It's a girl, anyway. I think."

"Flotsam? Jetsam?" said Luella, who knew her Disney movies inside and out.

"Aren't they the bad guy's familiars?"

"True." Her brow creased. "Brownie?"

Rose made a face.

"Cher," I said. "No, that's terrible. Garfunkel."

"It's a girl, remember?" said Luella.

"You two are categorically bad at naming otters," said Rose.

"Oh, yeah?" I said. "If you're so good at it, throw something in."

"Juliet. Ophelia."

I shook my head. "No Shakespeare."

We sat at the table where we'd left our things. The otter slipped into the pool and began swimming around happily, turning the occasional somersault.

"Let's see," I said. "We have Zephyr, Horatio, Princess; Chuck the squirrel and Arthur the bear; Crow—"

"Midnight," said Luella.

"Crow, AKA Midnight. Is that everybody's familiars that we know of?"

"Spiral," said Rose. "Tuesday's fire cat, remember?"

"Spiral, right."

"Maybe you're overthinking it," said Luella. "Don't worry so much about what everyone else named theirs; just name it what *you* want."

I blinked. "I guess I have trouble thinking of that first. Maybe I should take a closer look at her, see if it gives me any good ideas."

"Call 'er up."

I concentrated on the swimming otter, imagining her hopping out of the pool and coming over to us.

She ignored me completely and kept swimming. Her underwater path crossed and recrossed itself like a complicated knot.

"Knots!" I cried. "Boating knots! I got it." I waved a triumphant finger through the air. "Her name is Clove, like a clove hitch."

"Clove," mused Rose. "I like it."

I got up and knelt by the edge of the pool. "Clove," I said, softly, so my voice wouldn't carry too far.

The otters poked her head above water, then swam to the edge. She put her clawed paws over the edge and looked up at me with inquisitive eyes.

"You can play as long as you like—as long as you come when I call. Deal?"

Clove did an affirmative backwards roll into the water.

What a cutie.

I stood and rejoined my friends. "What do you say we pay Queenie a visit?"

Luella pushed back her chair and stood. "I'm dying to see this Fisher fellow."

"Me too," said Rose, joining us.

"What about your husband?" asked Luella.

"He'll be happy as a clam to hang out here for a few hours."

At Queenie's house, a Harley-Davidson motorcycle was parked in the driveway, with two helmeted figures just dismounting.

One of them pulled off her helmet and slammed it onto the seat. "That is the *last* time, Belinda Campbell, that I *ever* get a ride with you."

Luella's mother—known as "Mama" to everyone—pulled off her own helmet and grinned. "I thought you enjoyed yourself, Hilda, what with all the squealing you were doing."

"I wasn't squealing. I was screaming." Hilda Millefleur plucked at her gray hair, attempting to put it back in place. "I lost count of how many times you nearly killed us."

But Mama had stopped paying attention. "Hey, girl!" she called to Luella.

Luella hugged her mom. "Hey, Mama."

Mama released her and nodded to Rose and me. "How y'all doing?"

Hilda stalked over. "Tell your boyfriend," she said to Rose, "that he had better appreciate the day off he had today. I nearly died for it." She glared at Mama.

Mama clapped Hilda on the back and sent her stumbling a step. "Now, that's just plain not true. We had a good old time." Mama winked at Rose.

We walked to the front door.

Hilda pushed the button, and an old-fashioned gong rang out.

Fisher opened the door. He had exchanged his tie-dye "I Went to Sparkle Beach and All I Got Was This T-Shirt" shirt and Pete's swimming trunks for a colorful sarong and no shirt at all. He bowed deeply. "Lady witches."

Hilda's eyebrows shot up.

"Why, thank you kindly, young man," said Mama. She fluttered her hand like it was a lace fan.

"I'm not sure how young he is," I said.

Fisher straightened, with a model's perfect posture. "I am but one hundred years old."

Queenie swept in wearing an emerald green caftan. "Come, Fisher darling—show our guests to the lounge."

Fisher led the way.

Hilda addressed Queenie. "Does his age make him too young for you, or too old?"

"I think he's like the three bears' porridge," said Mama. "In between *too cold* and *too hot* is *just right*."

All three elder witches laughed.

"Mama!" said Luella, with a scandalized expression.

"What?" said Mama. "I'm just old. I ain't *dead*."

We seated ourselves on sleek couches around curvy space-age coffee tables. The lounge's tall windows overlooked the turquoise pool and the blue-gray river beyond.

Queenie adjusted the position of the clear glass water pitcher on the coffee table, then looked at me expectantly.

I looked around, waiting for someone else to start the meeting.

"This is your show, darling," said Queenie.

"But—aren't you . . . in charge?"

"Of course we are. But"—she gestured to the merman, who had settled on the floor, island-style, like he might break out a bongo at any moment—"Fisher came to you. These are your decisions to make."

I was in charge. Okay. I could do this. "Fisher, you said you couldn't tell me what favor your Queen wants, right?"

He made a half-bow from his sitting position. "That is so, Lady Pepper."

"So I have to go to the court of the Sweetwater Folk to find out. Where is the court?"

"It lies in the river deep."

"No, I mean, *where* exactly? Are we talking about the Intracoastal River? Is it near Sparkle Beach? Up the St. Johns River?"

Fisher tilted his head with an expression of polite confusion.

"I don't think he recognizes those names," said Hilda, dryly.

"How is she supposed to get there if she doesn't know where it is?" said Luella.

"I will guide her," said Fisher.

I shook my head. "Even if you're guiding me, I need a better idea of where this is than just 'out there.'"

"Perhaps this will help." Fisher rose and passed his hand over the water pitcher. Teal flashes shot through the water. A globe of water the size of a baseball rose from the container and floated in midair, catching the light streaming through the windows. He made another pass—and the ball of water transformed into a sparkling, turquoise-tinged impression of an intricately carved eye.

9

Rose gasped. "The magical eye! I threw that into a sulfur spring in the middle of the woods!"

The eye hovered above the water pitcher, rotating slowly as if staring at us all.

"It is as you say, Lady Rose. The Sweetwater Folk may be found beneath that same spring."

"So you all got the artifact, then?" said Mama.

"By the queen's decree, all that falls into our waters belongs to her."

"Not that," said Hilda, with razor sharp enunciation.

Fisher began to look nervous. The eye lost its shape as the water drizzled away into the pitcher like a fast-melting ice sculpture. "Lady witches, I—"

"Now look, you've made him upset," I said.

He cast me a grateful look. "I meant no harm, truly I did not." He looked down. "I should not have revealed it. My queen will likewise be displeased."

"Why?"

He paced like a darting fish, and pulled at his hair. "I have said too much. She will have my scales. She will show me no mercy, though I am her—" He froze and clapped his hand over his mouth.

"Her what?"

"Nothing. I meant nothing by it."

Mama gave Fisher a shrewd look.

Fisher muttered to himself in unintelligible chirps and squeaks.

"Fisher!" I clapped my hands. "Calm down."

He crossed the room in a blink, kneeled, and took my hand. Up close, he smelled of cypress and moss—and something with no scent, only the strange, fleeting impression of age, like the air inside a historic home. "We should leave now, before I say more."

"I'm sure she wouldn't be that hard on you—"

"She would. I swear it."

"I'll talk to her. Make her understand."

He shook his head. "No—"

I summoned my authoritative voice, long honed from dealing with Rocky and Kevin—and, occasionally, my husband. "I will go with you, but I can't rush into it. I have to be prepared. I promise I will speak for you."

He bowed his head. "So be it." He released my hand and returned to his spot on the floor. "That same spring in which the Lady Rose threw the jeweled eye is the closest portal to our court. I was instructed to bring you by a different way, one which you could not find again if not led—but if it will convince you to follow me, I will take you by way of the landmark you know."

"Underwater and underground," said Rose.

"How do you expect her to breathe?" asked Hilda.

"I will gate the waters such that she may walk rather than swim."

I shuddered. I wasn't claustrophobic, but an underwater cave was a whole new level of closed-in. "I'm not going alone," I said.

Fisher shifted. "I am commanded to bring the youngest . . ."

"Rose and Luella are as young as I am." I shot them a meaningful look.

"Definitely," said Rose.

"Oh, yes," added Luella. "Quite young."

"See?" I said to Fisher. "All three of us are the youngest. Problem solved."

Fisher bit his lip.

"Where *is* the jeweled eye?" said Hilda.

Fisher opened his mouth to speak.

Mama held up her hand to stop him. "Don't you go sharing that around. Never know when someone might try to find it a new home."

"I'm not a thief, if that's what you're implying," said Hilda.

"I didn't imply nothing. I just don't want this young man in any more trouble than he's already in."

Queenie waved a hand for silence. "It is settled. Pepper, Rose, and Luella will go below. We will wait by the spring until they return."

After our impromptu meeting at Queenie's house, I took Luella and Rose back to the resort. "You can hang out, you know, now that you're inside the gates."

Luella shook her head. "I'm too excited. I'm going home to get ready."

"Me too," said Rose.

We hugged goodbye, and I entered the lobby alone.

Upstairs, I opened the door to the sound of a TV playing at low volume.

Pete lay sprawled on the bed, still in his too-short bathrobe, sound asleep and snoring softly.

"Pete," I said, quietly so I didn't startle him. "Pete, wake up."

His eyes fluttered open. He smiled sleepily and reached for his glasses. "You're back."

I sat on the edge of the bed. "Did you have a nice nap?"

He yawned. "Best nap ever."

"Do you want to wake up a bit? I have some things to tell you about today."

He pushed himself up against the pillows. "I'm awake." He scooped up the TV remote and pressed the off button. "Tell me."

He listened without speaking while I retold the otter story and the conversation at Queenie's house.

"What do you think?" I said.

He had that serious look, the one he got when trying to figure out which movie he would place at the number one spot on his ever-changing list of favorite movies. "What do I think?" He rubbed his chin. "I think you're turning into quite a boss these days."

"A boss?"

"You know. 'Like a boss'? As in, 'I ate those chocolate pancakes like a boss.' Or, 'I summoned a magical otter like a boss.'"

"Like a boss," I echoed. I liked the way it sounded. "You don't think I'm getting in over my head?"

"Look," he said. "Mr. Merman—"

"Fisher."

"Whatever. You know me and names. He's a likeable sort, and if you're going with Luella and Rose, who are *also* apparently witches, how much safer could you be? It can't be any scarier than the Sparkle Beach Elementary parent pick-up loop."

I threw my arms around his neck. He smelled of hotel shampoo. "You're the best."

He stroked my hair. "Of course I am. Now stop hugging me before I decide to cancel sailing and find something even better to do."

I jumped up. "We're going sailing?"

"We're going sailing." He propped his hands behind his head, clearly pleased with himself. "I reserved us a rental."

"Well, come on, what are you doing lying around? Get up!" I pulled him by the arm.

He laughed. "I can't very well go in this bathrobe."

"Put your pants on and let's go!"

When he was finally dressed, we headed down to the bayside dock, where a sweet 22-footer awaited us. She had two sails—a jib and a mainsail—and graceful sleek curves.

I slipped on a nifty inflatable life jacket, the kind that automatically inflates in water, and Pete did the same. Then we boarded.

The boat rocked as we settled ourselves into our usual positions: Pete, as the crew, closer to the cabin; and me, as the helmsman, next to the tiller.

Although it was technically possible to sail away from the dock, it was kind of a pain in the butt. So I left the sails down and let the motor do the work of taking us out of the marina and into the bay.

When the water was deep enough, we lowered the keel and raised the motor. Pete swiftly raised the sails under my direction. The sails pulled tight as they caught the wind—and we were off!

I adjusted the tiller to bring us as close as possible to perpendicular to the wind, the fastest point of sail. If you've only ever been on a motorized boat, then you've only felt speed accompanied by the roaring whine of a motor. Under sail, speed is almost silent. When the sails are full, the boat slides through the water with a sensation halfway between gliding and flying. You hear only the rush of wind and the light prickle of water against the hull.

Pete caught my gaze and grinned. We were both feeling the adrenaline.

"Remember how to tack?" I said.

"I could tack in my sleep, Mrs. Monaco."

I chuckled and brought us closer to the wind. The tiller trembled like a living thing. A dark shadow in the distance meant a puff of wind was heading our way. As it raced across the surface of the bay, goosebumps appeared on the water's surface. The puff of wind blew over us and kept going.

"Ready about?" I said, using the verbal signal for beginning to tack.

Pete released the line holding the jib sheet in place. "Ready!"

"Hard-a-lee!" I turned the boat through the eye of the wind. I ducked the boom—marked *Hard Hat Area* for good reason—as it whipped across.

Pete ducked and shifted to the other side. He trimmed the sail as the boat surged forward on its new heading.

"You're a pretty good crew," I said. "I think I'll keep you." I said it as a joke, but it was true. You could sail solo, but having someone as crew made it so much easier. We made a good team.

Which reminded me that I was missing my newest crew member.

"Clove!" I called.

She appeared on the bow in a silver splash of magic that twinkled away into the sun like the spray from a breaking wave, her little nose to the wind.

"Is she here?" said Pete.

"She's on the bow."

Pete squinted in that direction.

Clove scrambled toward the cabin, stuck her head into the opening, and chirped with merry abandon.

"Now she's checking out the cabin," I said.

"Wish I could see her."

"Rose managed to show her sister her familiar," I said. "Maybe she could do the same for you."

Clove clambered down onto the empty seats across from Pete. Then she went on her hind legs, wrapping her silver claws around the lifeline, to peer across the bay.

The waves danced and slapped at the sides of the boat.

"Hey, Pep?"

"Hm?"

"Be careful tomorrow."

I kept my eyes on the water, looking for the next puff of wind. "Careful? Me? My middle name is 'Danger.' Pepper 'Danger' Monaco."

Without a word, he closed the space between us and kissed my cheek.

10

The morning light sliced through the branches and lit the pine needle-covered forest floor as Luella and Rose led the way into the woods behind the Nautilus County Fairgrounds. In one sense, the forest was an ordinary Florida scrub, no different than a thousand other patches of forest in or near Sparkle Beach—but the faint scent of rotten eggs brought back the stories my friends had told of the aftermath of the Circus Aetherium performance.

After a short walk, we entered a clearing. Beyond the clearing lay a milky green pool surrounded by columns made of rough beige stone. The stones themselves were made of thousands of tiny shell fragments. I pulled my shirt over my nose to block the smell, but it didn't help at all, so I tugged the t-shirt collar back down.

"Yoo-hoo, darlings." Queenie waved from a small white pop-up pavilion on the other side of the mint-green pond. "Over here." She managed to look ready for her close-up even in the middle of the woods, as if watching over a stinking spring while three witches and a merman descended into it was just another part of her glamorous day.

Luella gazed at the pool. "Sure looks different in the daytime."

Rose stopped and stared at the spring.

"Rose?" I said. "You coming?"

"Yeah." It was like her feet had been stuck to the ground. When she finally walked on, her face had a troubled look.

Fisher popped out of the pavilion with a wave. He had on Pete's trunks again, and a Suntan Queen t-shirt that Queenie must have dug up somewhere. "Good morning, lady witches!"

"No one should be that cheerful this early," said Rose.

Luella elbowed her. "I think it's sweet."

"You would."

"So how do we get down below?" I asked.

Queenie gestured toward the spring. "Fisher says they have magical gates to block the water from the passageways—but to descend to the passageways, you and I must lift out the springwater."

My eyes widened. "Lift out? As in levitate?"

She nodded.

"And then all that goes over us once we're inside? How do we get back out?"

"You'll pass through the gate and swim up," said Queenie. "It's only about eight feet deep."

Luella made a face. "It sure does smell."

"So will we," said Rose.

I sighed. "Guess that hotel shower's going to get another workout." I bounced on the balls of my feet, trying to cover for the fact that I was starting to feel nervous. "Let's do this thing. Fisher?"

He made a slight bow. "Lady Pepper."

We surrounded the pool.

Queenie rubbed her ring-covered fingers together. "We will lift from either side. Once you enter, I will take over holding the load. It's the first lift that's tricky to do alone."

"Got it." I shook out my arms and did a few quick lunges and squats.

"What are you doing?" said Rose.

"This is my surf warmup. Should work for climbing down rocks, too." I finished the last few stretches. "Ready, Queenie."

"All right, darling." She stretched her hands toward the milky green water.

I did the same.

Our magic sparked into being from both sides of the pond. Silver glittered across the green surface and sank into the water. When our combined magic had enveloped the entire pond, I pushed the water up and felt Queenie do the same.

The water rose and floated in the air like it was in a too-full cup, spilling over the top of our magical container and showering the stones below. Natural rings of limestone descended to a black hole at the bottom of the empty spring.

"You can let go," said Queenie.

"Are you sure?"

She nodded.

I slowly released most of my hold on the water, although I kept a little awareness in reserve in case Queenie's hold slipped. Nobody wants a metric ton of water to fall on their head.

Fisher climbed down the stones with light, quick steps.

Rose smirked. "He makes it look easy."

Luella marched forward and sat on an exposed ledge. "Did you ever go down the stairs on your butt when you were a kid?" She scooted down the ledge and landed on the next one down.

Rose took a step into the empty spring and stopped. "It's still wet."

I rolled my eyes. "It's a *spring*, what do you expect?"

She took one step down, then another. "Maybe it's the fire witch in me."

I left the bank and stepped onto the rough, wet stone. The smell of sulfur was stronger than ever. I carefully made my way down until I stood with Fisher, Luella, and Rose over the black opening at the bottom of the spring. "You first," I said to Fisher.

Fisher stepped into the tight space and took a few uneven steps downward. Each time, he appeared to get shorter and shorter, until only his head was showing. Then he used his hands to grip the opening and lower himself the rest of the way down.

The green water floated above our heads like a flawed emerald filtering the sunlight.

Luella, Rose, and I looked at each other.

"I'll go next," I said. I followed Fisher into the darkness. Each step made the stones feel tighter around my body until the movement of air showed I'd fully entered some sort of open chamber beneath the spring itself.

Luella came next, blocking out the green light from above.

I moved aside and bumped into Fisher. "You guys have any lights down here?"

Cool green light traced across the walls in flowing curlicues, lighting up the space. The chamber measured perhaps twenty feet across, with an opening to the side leading off in another direction.

Fisher had his hand on the wall. "Is this suitable?"

"How'd you do that?" I traced my fingers on the cold stone.

"We have our own magic, lady witch."

"I'll say," said Luella, who had stepped all the way down and joined us. She looked around at the glowing walls. "Green, not silver."

Rose came down last. She had conjured her cat, Horatio, who now rode on her shoulders like a furry black scarf. In the low light, his golden eyes flashed with suspicion.

The water sank until it covered the chamber opening, blocking out all but a faint glow of sunlight. The chamber was silent but for our quiet breath and a far-off *drip drip drip*.

"If you would follow me, please," Fisher said.

I stepped forward.

Luella and Rose crowded close.

When we left the sulfur spring chamber, Fisher lit the passageway wall with a touch of his hand. Sand, rock fragments, and tiny shells crunched beneath our feet.

I glanced back, and the sulfur spring chamber fell into darkness behind us. I swallowed a sudden lump in my throat, returned my gaze forward, and kept walking. "How far?"

"Not far," said Fisher. His voice echoed in the tube-like hallway.

"What are these lights?" said Rose.

"They are part of our magic."

"I get that," said Rose, "but how do they work?"

Fisher continued walking without speaking for a few moments. "Magic belongs to the queens. They placed these lights long ago."

"And the gates?" said Luella.

"The same."

"When you say 'queens,' do you mean a long line of queens? Or do you have more than one at a time?" said Rose. Horatio added a soft meow.

"It is . . . complicated," said Fisher.

Rose huffed exasperation into the chilled air. "I hate it when men say that."

"Forgive me, Lady Fire Witch."

She made a sound of amusement. "That's my new title," she said, slightly mollified. "Remember that when we get out of here."

We walked on. Fisher lit up each new passageway we took. The air lost its sulfur smell and took on a fresher aroma of minerals and moss.

"Where is everyone?" said Luella.

"They are already called to assemble." Fisher paused. "Would you permit me to stop at my chamber? It is not far from our path."

We followed him down a smaller tunnel and through an opening in the rock, which revealed a cozy chamber about the size of Queenie's swimming pool.

"This is your room?" Luella looked around. "Where's your bed?"

"He doesn't have a bed, silly," said Rose. "Usually this would be filled with water. Right, Fisher?"

"As you say, Lady Rose." Fisher touched something tied to the wall—instead of shelves, personal items were secured with bits of twine, rope, or salvaged chain. A knot came loose under his fingers, releasing a string of small jagged crystals that sparkled in the green-tinged light. He placed it around his neck and re-tied it. "I will be expected to wear this," he said, with a touch of apology in his tone.

"No problem," I said. "What else you got in here?"

Fisher looked pleasantly surprised. "You wish to see?" He glanced around as if he didn't know where to start. He stooped to touch a large hunk of rusty metal with three fin shapes radiating out from the center. "This is from the upper river. I believe it is part of one of your human boats." He stood and seized a glass bottle tied to the wall by its neck. "This makes music." He blew across the neck of the bottle and the resulting tone reverberated around the chamber.

"How lovely," said Luella, with her usual Southern manners.

Horatio jumped down from Rose's shoulder and began nosing around the items on the floor.

Rose picked up a heavy-looking item shaped like a belt. "What's this?"

"It's a diving belt," I said. "Keeps you underwater."

Fisher carefully took it from Rose. "I once dropped this relic on my toes, when I was in human form by the upper river."

The three of us took a respectful step back while Fisher neatly folded and replaced the belt. Then he led the way out of the chamber and into the passageway.

We continued walking, with Rose's cat at our heels. Farther on, we reached a larger opening covered with what looked like a hanging bead curtain—except the beads were made of tiny stones, like Fisher's bracelets and necklace.

Fisher stopped and faced us. "We are here."

"Should you go in and let them know?" said Luella.

Fisher regarded her with solemn eyes. "She knows."

"Should I say anything special?" I looked to my friends. "How's my hair?"

"You never worry about your hair," said Rose.

My hand went to the pearl on my necklace. Suddenly, I didn't want to step through alone, even if my friends were right behind me. "Hang on a sec." I pictured my otter. "Clove, baby—where are you?"

The otter's paws crunched across the crushed shell floor as she ran up to my side. She romped around my legs, shaking off magic like glitter, then settled for poking her nose repeatedly into the stone bead curtain.

I knelt and gave Clove a reassuring pat. I'm not sure she needed it—but I did.

"I feel left out," said Luella. "Zephyr!"

The air moved, making the stone beads clatter against each other.

Luella's white and silver dog appeared in a gust of wind at her side.

"Much better," said Luella. "Carry on."

Fisher held aside the curtain.

Beyond lay only blackness.

I stepped through with Clove beside me.

11

The lights that blazed to life outshone Fisher's glowing cave tracings like a lighthouse outshines a pocket flashlight. I shielded my eyes with my arm. Green afterimages zipped across my vision. "Hey, dial it back!"

The blinding light dimmed.

I peeked out.

I had just shouted at the hundreds of people who filled what I could now see was an absolutely enormous cave.

The people standing in the cave were not what anyone would describe as fully clothed. Instead, they had draped themselves with bits of plant material—lily pads here, ferns there—without seeming to notice whether it covered anything important. The shifting green light created the illusion that all of us were underwater.

Clove peered around my ankle and made a few curious peeps.

The merpeople glided into small formations facing us. One woman raised a rattle and shook it.

At the sound, the Sweetwater Folk began to move in a slow-motion dance, like an ancient Egyptian painting come to life—all formal steps and elegant poses. Their faces remained composed as they solemnly wove between each other, ending in a group bow facing the far end of the cave, where water trickled from a massive stalactite.

"There's a truly unfortunate lack of pants in here," said Luella, quiet enough so her words wouldn't carry.

The trickle from the stalactite became a stream, then a gushing roar that pounded the cave floor below. Instead of pooling, the water formed the shape of a clear liquid throne, flowing and shifting and reflecting the light like a diamond.

Another watery shape formed above the seat of the throne. The indistinct shape separated and solidified into the form of a woman. Streams of water from her head turned into long, tangled locks. Garlands of rough crystals draped her head, neck, wrists, and ankles, and a patchwork of dewy wetland flowers draped her from shoulder to ankle.

The water from the roof of the cave no longer gushed, but fell softly like rain over the Sweetwater Queen. She lifted a single finger.

The assembled people straightened from their collective bow.

Except for Fisher, the merpeople around us transformed in the blink of an eye into water, collapsing into puddles where they had stood only a second previous. The water flowed away through hidden cracks and crevices until the cave stood empty but for the throne, the queen, and us.

Horatio lifted his paw with distaste, as if there might be merpeople water on it. Zephyr barked. Clove just hopped back and forth.

"The merpeople are okay, right?" I asked Fisher, while keeping my eyes on the queen.

"They are well, only transformed," Fisher replied.

The queen swept us with a gaze like starlight on water.

Fisher bowed. "My Mother," he said, "I have brought the youngest witch."

Luella, Rose, and I traded glances.

"Mother?" I said.

The queen ignored me. "Who are the others?" Her voice flowed like serene water, smooth and light, almost melodious.

"They are also the youngest witches."

She moved her ancient gaze over us. "Rise. You have completed your task."

Fisher straightened.

"Step forward, young witch."

I glanced at Luella and Rose before taking a step forward like I was playing a high-stakes game of Mother, May I.

"There has been no contact between our Folk and yours for many years. We are pleased you have made the journey. We would like to present a gift, as a token of our thanks." The queen rose, her flower gown fluttering in the continuous drizzle, and removed a single purple flower from her dress. The airborne water droplets followed her as she stepped forward and placed the flower in my hair. Her eyes flickered with green light. "Now we grant you leave to return to your home."

The queen turned away and glided back to her throne.

"Wait—what? What about the favor you wanted?"

She sank into the water throne with graceful unconcern. "When there is a dispute with the Saltwater Folk, it is required only that a negotiator is summoned. We have done our part. Now the matter may rest." She nodded to Fisher. "Return the witch to her proper place."

"My Mother, I—"

"Silence."

Fisher bowed his head.

I put my hands on my hips. "Um, excuse me?"

The queen turned her strange, green-tinged gaze to me.

Fisher looked up, and his eyes widened like I'd done something very bad.

I ignored his look and kept going. "So . . . you interrupted my vacation and had me dragged down some stinky tunnel just to tell me you didn't need me anyway and I should go *home*?"

The queen tilted her head to the side like an osprey spotting prey.

Luella put her hand on my shoulder. "Maybe we should just go—"

I shook her off. "And all I got for it was a *flower*?"

Green light played over the queen's skin. Her liquid throne stilled like it had turned to ice. Then her mouth twitched—and she laughed, high and brittle as crystal. The laugh bounced through the chamber.

Fisher appeared to be deep breathing, or possibly hyperventilating.

The queen leaned forward. Flower petals broke away from her gown and swirled away through the watery throne. "We are the Sweetwater Queen. We owe you nothing."

"Oh, yeah? Well, I'm a Ride-or-Die Witch, and I think you're full of crap."

Fisher covered his face with his hands.

The queen rose from the throne. Flowers fell from her makeshift covering. She opened her mouth like she was going to scream. Clear water fountained out of it; at the same time, she opened her hands and released a firehose blast of water from each palm.

"Good Lord," said Luella.

I waited. I had plenty of experience with temper tantrums—mine and other people's.

The water stopped gushing from the queen's mouth and hands.

"You finished?" I said.

Fisher peeked out from between his fingers.

"You are still here," said the queen. "Did we not frighten you?"

"I'm a water witch. Water's my thing. Just because you shot it out of your piehole doesn't mean I'm going to run and hide."

The queen subsided into her throne. The flowing throne water caught her hair and pulled it into its current. She didn't seem to notice. Instead, she stared into the distance. "Our son wishes us to negotiate."

Fisher lowered his hands and looked at me with guarded hope.

"For what?"

"For that which was stolen from our waters."

Now we were getting somewhere. "What was it, and who stole it?"

The queen idly, almost lovingly, traced her finger through the arm of the water throne. "The Saltwater Folk stole a human from the green spring."

Rose, Luella, and I traded alarmed looks. "What human?" I said. "What was her name?"

"We know not," said the queen.

"Why did they kidnap her?"

"We know not."

I wanted to shake her by her shoulders. "What *do* you know?"

"By rights, the human is ours. It is a grave offense on the part of the Saltwater Folk. But it is not the only prize that fell into the spring that night."

"The artifact," said Rose.

The queen scooped a handful of water from the arm of her throne and released it to float in front of her. It shifted and formed the shape of an eye. "Our son," she continued, "has a dangerous fondness for things above. He has made human friends before, and seeks another opportunity to repeat his folly. He would save this human."

Fisher raised his head with a flash of defiance in his eyes.

"Save her from what?" said Luella.

"From death," said the queen, with calm unconcern.

"They're going to *kill* her?" said Rose.

"She is human. She cannot thrive below the sea."

I lifted Clove from the ground and held her close. She tickled my cheek with her whiskers. "Why not let me negotiate? What do you have to lose?"

"Her pride," said Fisher. "She would not lower herself to treat with the Saltwater Queen, though it is the old custom."

"Silence!" cried the queen. The floating water eye dropped to the ground with a splash. The queen stood and struck the throne. Like the eye, it collapsed into a flood beneath her feet. With a flash of green-tinged magic, she lifted the mass of water and flung it at her son.

Fisher reeled from the impact, but recovered, dripping with water. He gazed at the queen with pain in his eyes. "You should not fight one another."

"She broke the peace," spat the queen, pacing the natural stone dais.

"The two of you haven't been at peace since I was a child!"

She froze.

"And you would tear me apart as well, if only you could."

In the silence after his words, only the falling droplets from the stalactites made noise.

12

I set Clove down. "Wait a minute. I thought this was a fight over what fell into the spring—you kept an artifact, and the other queen kept a person. Why would you tear Fisher apart?"

Fisher turned to me. "Lady Pepper, what your boon companion is to you—"

I glanced at my left hand, where my wedding band caught the green light. "Pete? He's my husband."

Fisher nodded. "So the Sweetwater and the Saltwater Queen are to each other."

I slapped my forehead. "Oh! They're *married*. And you're their *son*. And all they do is fight?"

"It is so, Lady Pepper." He glanced at the Sweetwater Queen, and then lifted his chin. "They are *both* my Mothers. I cannot side with one or the other, but only wish for peace."

Rose scratched her fire cat's fuzzy head. "This is why I'm never getting married, Horatio. Too much drama."

"Fisher," said Luella, "would the Saltwater Queen really harm the person she kidnapped?"

The queen opened her mouth.

"Don't even think about it," I said. "We've had enough fire hoses for one day. Go on, Fisher."

"I do not believe she would do so intentionally, but they are . . . wild, by nature."

"Feral sea criminals," said the Queen.

"You married one," said Rose.

The Queen shot her a look of silent, green-glowing fury.

"Aha!" cried Fisher. "See?"

"We see nothing." The queen crossed her arms in a very human-like gesture, crushing the mantle of flowers over her front.

I put my hands on my hips. "You summoned me here—all this way—just to say you'd done your part, didn't you? That's all it was. You made the gesture of recruiting a witch to negotiate but you never had any intention of following through. You were going to keep your magical artifact and let her keep her captive, all the while refusing to speak to each other and making your son miserable in the process."

She wouldn't look at me. Instead, she toyed with a wet lock of hair.

"Well, listen, sister. I don't play that way. Neither one of you has the right to keep a person as a pet, so we're sorting this out—and we're sorting it out *right now*."

The queen examined her moss-colored fingernails. "We don't have to listen to you."

"Oh, yes, you do. Unless you want these caves turned into a tourist attraction—"

"What is a tourist attraction?" said Fisher.

"People tramping through here every hour on the hour," said Luella.

Fisher brightened.

The queen glowered.

"Then you had better help us get to that stolen human and *get her back*." I summoned my magic to gather the water from the floor. I shaped it into a throne and sat, using my powers to float on it—and to keep the water from seeping through my clothes. It was already chilly enough in the cave.

Rose ignited balls of fire in her hands and stepped to my right side, flanked by her fire cat and his flame-tipped tail. Luella summoned gusts of air and stepped to my left, with Zephyr at her side. Our glittering silver magic swirled through the fire, wind, and water.

Clove hopped back and forth, squeaking triumphantly.

"We are the Ride-or-Die Witches," I said, "and we don't mess around."

The queen stilled. In the shifting green light, she resembled an ancient statue carried away from its home: beautiful and lonely, powerful and sad. She picked up one of her crystal garlands and caressed the single shell attached to the strand. She rubbed the shell against her cheek before letting it fall back into the tangle of garlands and flowers. She bowed her head. "We will permit you to negotiate on our behalf."

I stood. I lifted the water throne with my magic and floated it to the queen. "Here," I said. "This is yours."

She sank into it and nodded to Fisher, who stepped forward. "You have our permission to guide them to the Saltwater Court."

"As you wish, my Mother." He bowed.

The queen's gaze swept over Rose, Luella, and me. "Fare you well, Ride-or-Die Witches. Tell the Saltwater Queen—" She paused and caressed the shell again. "Tell her: I remember the bay, where once we met in peace." Her body turned to water in the shape of a woman, then blended with the water of the throne. All of it sank gently to the floor and disappeared into the crevices, leaving her mantle of flowers strewn across the rocks. The green light from the walls dimmed to a softer glow.

Clove bounded forward to the abandoned dais as if she might find the queen hidden in one of the many crevices. Zephyr followed, swishing her tail while she nosed around the cave floor.

I elbowed Fisher. "So you're the heir of two kingdoms?"

"He's the world's most eligible mer-bachelor," said Rose.

Fisher turned bashful. "I have yet to choose a mate."

"He's going to be a hit with the mer-singles," said Luella with a wink.

In the green light, it was impossible to see if Fisher blushed—but he hurried out of the chamber without making eye contact. We followed him and navigated the glowing tunnels back to the sulfur spring.

The green water loomed overhead.

Clove hopped around excitedly.

I gestured to the familiars. "What are these guys going to do? Do Zephyr and Horatio swim?"

"There's no danger," said Luella. "They have their own mysterious ways of getting around."

"They'll show up again wherever we go," added Rose.

I nodded. Knowing that the familiars would take care of themselves was a relief. I put my hands on my hips and eyed the opening above us. "Couldn't I lift out the water again? Then we could stay dry."

"Don't," said Rose. "You might pull something if you try it by yourself."

"Ugh. Sulfur swim it is. Here goes nothing." I climbed the rocks until I reached the top of the spring chamber. I pushed my hand into the water. It sealed around my wrist, and closed smoothly when I withdrew my hand. I took several deep breaths to build up my oxygen supply. Then I held my breath, swiftly climbed upward into the water, and pushed off from the bottom of the spring.

A few strong strokes brought me to the surface. I gasped the sulfur-scented air and swept my soaking wet hair out of my face.

Queenie rose from her camp chair and hurried to the edge of the spring.

"I'm fine," I said. "Luella and Pepper are right behind me." I swam a little ways until my feet could touch the upward sloping edge of the pool. The purple flower floated free and spun away across the rippling surface.

Queenie reached for my arm and helped me climb out. "What did they want, darling?"

"It's complicated," I said.

Luella popped up from the center of the pond.

I used my magic to gather the water on my clothes and hair into a ball, and then I dropped the ball of water in the spring with a splash. When Luella got to the bank, I did the same for her.

Rose came up next, scowling. "This reeks." She swam over to us and climbed out.

I dried her off.

Queenie reeled back a few steps and waved her hand in front of her face. "Darlings, you need a shower."

I attempted to fluff my curls, but they were misbehaving thanks to the minerals left behind by the spring water. "Showers will have to wait. I need to get in touch with Mrs. Millefleur."

13

Gladys, the purple-haired receptionist for Millefleur Properties, led me down the hall and into Hilda Millefleur's office. "She'll be with you in a moment, dear." She winked, then pulled the door closed.

I settled into one of the armchairs facing the massive wooden desk.

I'd missed most of the excitement with Mrs. Millefleur, starting with the lighthouse incident and continuing with the aftermath of the first disastrous Circus Aetherium performance. While the others raced to Mrs. Millefleur's beachside mansion, I dutifully gathered my family and headed home. Later on, when Rose, Luella, Oliver, and Mrs. Millefleur confronted Lenore in the woods after the second circus performance, I went with the other group and missed the whole thing.

Hearing about it later wasn't quite the same.

Now Rose got to call the elder fire witch by her first name, as if it were some kind of great privilege, and I didn't even know if I trusted the woman.

Strike that. I *knew* I didn't trust her.

The water cooler in the back corner let out a belching gurgle, and then the door opened.

Hilda Millefleur entered, looking crisp and professional in a crimson skirt and jacket.

I brushed uselessly at my wrinkled, sulfur-scented clothes.

She sat behind the desk and folded her hands. "Where are the other two?"

"The other two?"

"I assumed you came in a set of three."

Nice. She wasn't being subtle about implying that I wasn't good enough to handle this by myself. "I told them to go home and change."

She pursed her lips, then sighed.

It wasn't what anyone would call a vote of confidence, but I had no choice but to go ahead and tell her the full story of the cave trip anyway. "It has to be Lenore. She disappeared in the spring at the same time as the artifact."

"I would assume so." She made a tiny adjustment to the position of an expensive-looking pen on her desk. "I fail to see how this affects me."

My mouth fell open. "You're not serious. I mean, I know you haven't exactly mounted a huge rescue effort since she vanished, but now we have a lead on where she is."

"My sister can take care of herself."

"You want to leave your sister in the hands of some random bunch of sea people who may leave her to drown the second they lose interest? As long as she's not drowning right in front of you, you're okay with it?"

Mrs. Millefleur sat as still as a sailboat on a windless lake. "Did I say that?"

"Sure sounded like you did."

"Your listening comprehension is poor."

"Poor? *Poor*? If my sister were trapped under the sea, I'd—"

"Spare me. Firstly, you have no idea of the nature of the relationship between my sister and me. Secondly, I suspect she has her own way out, and has chosen not to use it."

"How could you possibly know that?"

"Because I gave it to her."

"You *what*?"

"Your listening comprehension *is* poor. I gave her a way out." She paused. "I gave her an artifact."

I blinked. "No . . . you told us she *stole* the magical eye."

"She did."

I stared at her. None of this made any sense.

"The artifact I'm referring to is not the stolen Eye of the Elements. That, my sister stole on her own time, and lost when Rose took it and threw it in the spring. No, the artifact I gave her is quite different."

"What does it do?"

"It allows her to travel into the Shadows."

All at once, the story I'd been told about that night re-arranged itself. I banged my hands on her desk. "You knew she had two artifacts all along. You let us think it was some great mystery!"

"No one was hurt."

"No one was hurt? *That's* your justification?"

She widened her eyes innocently. "You see? I'm not a monster. I would not abandon my sister to a 'random bunch of sea people,' as you put it."

I scoffed. "Is it because you're richer than the rest of us that you think you can do anything you want and get away with it? Or is it because you're an arrogant—"

"Don't you like being a witch?"

"Of course I—" I crossed my arms. "Don't change the subject."

"Admit it. This brings interest to your pedestrian life."

"Like you know anything about my life."

"Walk away," she countered. "Go back to your quaint little existence. Lenore will be fine."

Quaint little existence. What a freaking psychopath. "I wasn't trying to get *out* of it; I promised the Sweetwater Queen I'd negotiate, and I was asking for your *help*."

"I have better things to do than try to rescue my idiot sister, who, for the record, most likely doesn't need rescuing."

"Hang on a minute. If you gave her an artifact, then why did she track you down and try to make you give her your magic, too? Wouldn't she have been happy you were willing to help her?"

A faint smile lifted one corner of her lips. "She doesn't know the Key came from me."

"How could she not know?"

Mrs. Millefleur relaxed into the chair as if recalling a pleasant memory. "I hypnotized her. She always wanted to be a witch, so I planted a spellbook in her belongings, and suggested that she must hold onto it at all costs—and that if she were ever in great need, she must cast the spell in it that called for an enchanted key. Then I created a listing for an enchanted key on an auction website. No one else would have bought such a thing, and if they had, I would have cancelled the transaction. The moment my sister bought it, I knew the suggestion had been activated."

"But your sister must have been in big trouble, then."

"Fired, bankrupt, and desperate, yes."

"So you thought you'd just toss her a random magical artifact and she'd be fine?"

"My sister's a fool, but she's not stupid. I knew she would figure out how to put it to use. And she did."

"Right," I said. "By stealing another magical artifact and then threatening you and Rose into giving up your powers."

Mrs. Millefleur shrugged. "She is *my* sister, after all."

"You two need therapy."

"We're too old for that."

"You're never too old. You think you're not going to need some advanced conflict resolution when she finds out you've been pulling her strings all along?"

"I am not afraid of Lenore."

"Liar. If you weren't afraid of her, you wouldn't have pushed Luella, Rose, and me into taking her on for you."

Her eyes flashed. "I confronted her alone, after the second performance of the Circus Aetherium. *Alone.* Without any of you."

"That worked well, did it?" I silently pulled a stream of water out of the water cooler and collected it behind Mrs. Millefleur where she wouldn't see it. "Don't glower at me. I've been glowered at enough today, by far scarier than the likes of you. You can clean up your own mess. You're coming with me whether you want to or not, and you're going to *talk* to your sister once and for all, and *end* this."

"What makes you think I would do that?"

"Because you're not the only one who can make threats, and I'm not settling for anything less than getting the Key and the Eye into safe hands. Not yours, and not Lenore's. If you don't step up, I'll knock your house off its foundations. And if I'm in a *good* mood, I might do it when you're not at home."

"You wouldn't dare—"

I silently moved the globe of water over her head. The liquid I'd pulled from the cooler would be enough to drench her iron-gray hair, her fine suit, and the leather chair. "Try me."

I let the water go.

She snapped her fingers.

The water boiled away to steam in an instant.

Not a drop of liquid had touched her.

She laughed, causing the vapor-filled air to swirl. "You want to galavant off and rescue my sister? How could anyone take you seriously when all you have are parlor tricks? What *has* Queenie been teaching you?"

"She's been teaching me a lot."

"Like what?"

"Well, surfing . . ."

Mrs. Millefleur rolled her eyes.

"And other stuff! Water manipulation—"

"Dropping water on people's heads?"

I ignored the crack and kept going. "Mood reading. Blood is water, so I can tell when someone's heartbeat is fast. My familiar finally showed up, too." I shot her a venomous look. "I'm sorry it's not as impressive as what Rose or Luella can do."

She waved a hand dismissively. "Apologies don't suit you. Your problem isn't in your natural abilities or in Queenie's training; it's in your reluctance to think big enough."

"What, like you? I'm not throwing enough people off lighthouses? Not mailing enough dangerous artifacts to my estranged relatives?"

"So defensive. If you would calm down, you'd see I'm right. You talk a good game—but you're afraid of your own power."

"I—" The instinct to snap back collided with a stabbing sensation in my stomach.

"Luella was too gentle, and had to be driven to reach her potential. Rose was too skittish, and had to be soothed. You've always known what your own problem is, haven't you?"

I toyed with the pearl on my necklace and didn't meet her gaze.

"That's why your familiar took so long to show up—and why it finally did."

"Because of Fisher."

"Not Fisher, personally. What Fisher represented: a challenge. Something worthy of the witch you know you are inside." She folded her hands. "I will make you a deal.

Bring back my sister, and I promise I will settle this once and for all."

Her face looked calm, but beneath her skin, her blood rushed and fluttered. Was she nervous about her sister, me, or something else entirely? There was no way to know—but there was only one answer I could give.

"Deal," I said.

14

The hammock swung back and forth thanks to a push from Pete's foot. I closed my eyes and let the world rock while the sea breeze brushed over my skin. "I feel like I spent yesterday just threatening people. First the mermaid queen. Then Mrs. Millefleur." I opened my eyes and peered at my husband to see his reaction. I'd already told him the full story, but it was my right as a married person to retell my stories to my spouse as many times as I wanted to. The trade-off was that I had to listen to my spouse's stories as many times as he wanted to tell them.

Pete shifted in the hammock, where we lay head-to-toe, balancing each other out. "It's something you're good at."

I smiled and rested my arm over my eyes to block the light of the rising sun. "No, it isn't. And if you say that again, I'll dump you out of this hammock."

"You just made my point. Has it ever struck you as weird that she insists on being called 'Mrs. Millefleur' instead of Hilda?"

I laughed. "I wouldn't call her Hilda, even if she asked me—not for all the pearls in Tahiti. Hold on, I'm going to get up. I don't think the waves are going to get any better than they are right now."

He grabbed the edge of the hammock and held on as I rolled up and stood. "I'm going to stay right here in this hammock and watch." He adjusted his Ray-Ban sunglasses. "Put on a good show for me, will you?"

I gave the hammock a teasing push, nearly flipping him over the side, before issuing him a mock salute. "Yes, sir." I walked off and grabbed my board.

Surfing was just what I needed to clear my head.

Before I was even a water witch, almost every sunrise found me riding the waves. Workday, weekend, it didn't matter. I needed my fix; I needed to fly in the only way I knew how. Adding magic to the water just made me want it more.

The waves at the beach beside the Vivacqua weren't as good as the ones to the north, at the inlet between the jetties—but on the right day, with the right tide, I could do pretty well. As long as there weren't any sharks nipping around. Sparkle Beach had the dubious honor of being the shark bite capital of the world.

I paddled out and rode the swells, watching for a likely wave.

There's an art to it, reading a wave. Some waves break to the surfer's left, others to the surfer's right. Those you ride in the direction of the break. Some waves break all at once, leaving you no option but to jet forward as the wave crashes behind you.

If you're skilled, and you're lucky, you catch a few moments of pure heaven. If you're not, you end up in the washing machine.

Either way, you get back up on your board and do it all over again.

Pete resembled a tiny doll onshore, mostly visible by his bright straw fedora and the length of his legs stretched out in the hammock.

I caught a few small waves, then paddled to a likelier looking spot in hopes of finding a larger one.

The lumps on the horizon seemed more uneven than usual. They swelled closer and larger, but instead of transforming into waves, they maintained their individuality as hills of water.

Strange. I'd never seen a pattern like that before.

I turned and tried paddling toward shore. The current sucked me backward toward the open water. The pull was too broad and too strong to counteract with water magic; all I could do was try to paddle sideways like it was a rip current.

The hills collapsed on themselves unlike any natural wave I'd ever seen.

A tinge of anxiety crawled over my skin. Something was off.

The sea around me went glassy calm for the count of five.

Then, a dozen human hands reached out of the water and landed on my surfboard. I should have screamed; all I could think was *At least it's not a shark.* The bubbling sound of underwater laughter came from below as the hands gripped the edges of the board. Some of the nails were dyed blue, the color of a bruise. With a surge of motion, they flung the board upward.

I flew into the air like I'd taken a badly judged trampoline jump. A silhouette of a fish appeared below me just before I hit the water and plunged into the murky depths.

Panic disappeared, replaced by an odd sense of calm. I'd been thrown in the washing machine a thousand times— what made this any different? The large shapes swimming around me?

I could summon only a distant sense of annoyance that Pete might be worried if he saw me wipe out. I floated in the churn, weightless, finding my bearings as seconds passed like slow-motion heartbeats.

The sun penetrated the water. The murky light revealed flashing fins, seaweed hair, and free-floating ropes of shells.

The Saltwater Folk.

I kicked hard and broke the surface. I kept my head and breathed deeply, to build up oxygen in case they tried to send me under again.

They surfaced. Some of them smiled, showing teeth the color of old ivory behind lips the same bruised blue I'd spotted on their nails. Their kelp-like hair floated on the surface.

I was surrounded.

"Go away," one of them said.

"Yes, go away," another echoed.

"Never come back!"

"Never!"

They burst into wild laughter and dove beneath the surface.

I kicked in a circle trying to see where they'd gone, but they'd disappeared. My surfboard floated a few feet away, still tethered by the surf leash attached to my ankle. A few strokes brought it within reach, and then I paddled back to shore.

Pete had fallen asleep in the hammock with his hat on his face.

I moved his hat. "Fat lot of help you were. Your wife gets ambushed by mermaids and all you can do is snooze." There wasn't any heat in my words, though. I was glad he hadn't seen. He might have panicked. I had handled it all by myself anyway.

Pete sighed and smiled in his sleep.

I ruffled his hair. "Hey, you."

"'S nice," he murmured. "Do it again."

"Open your eyes and I'll think about it."

He cracked his eyelids and winced, then adjusted his Ray-Bans.

"How am I supposed to know if your eyes are open?"

He pulled the shades down and winked.

"Goofball," I said, ruffling his hair again.

He took advantage of my leaned-over position to grab me by the wrist and pull me into the hammock, wet bathing suit and all.

I shrieked as the hammock unbalanced and dumped both of us on the sand. He landed on the bottom; I landed on top.

Silent laughter shook his whole body, which shook me, thanks to our sandwiched position.

"You—you—"

He smiled while I sputtered. "Call me 'goofball' again, I was kind of digging it," he said.

"Argh!" I grabbed his shirt collar and gave him a good shake. I had places to go, things to do—and I probably should have mentioned the salty mermaids I'd encountered—but his gaze was too warm and too lively for me to think about all that.

So I kissed the hell out of him instead.

15

"There's just one problem," Pete said when we came up for air. "Who's going to pilot your party cruise? I mean, they're *Saltwater* Folk—they're going to be in the ocean."

I slapped myself in the head. "I didn't even think of that! You and I are only rated for inland boats."

"And you can't hire a charter."

"Obviously. 'Hi, Captain, we're going to sail out to meet the merpeople. Wanna come?'"

"So what are you going to do?"

"Time for an all-call." I pulled out my phone and composed a message to the entire group of Sparkle Beach witches, except for Mrs. Millefleur, who thought texting was for barbarians. *Do any of you have a sea captain's license?*

The negative answers arrived quickly.

"What am I going to do, Pete? Even I can't swim out that far."

"Maybe the mermaids can come to you."

The phone pinged.

"Wait—here's Oliver."

I have the proper license, he wrote.

You never told me you were a boat captain, Rose replied.

You never asked, said Oliver.

I looked up from the phone. "Apparently, Oliver's a sea captain."

"He's a real James Bond type, isn't he?" said Pete.

The phone rang while I was still holding it in my hand. "It's my dad." I scrambled out of the sand and stood up. "Hi, Dad. Is everything okay?"

"Everything is fine. The boys wanted to watch *Seinfeld*, but I thought I should ask you first."

I chuckled. "They were trying to put one over on you. They always want to watch it because Pete and I watch it, but I haven't found a single episode yet that doesn't have something a little too grown-up in it. There's always the one line that ruins it. Well, except for maybe 'The Soup Nazi.'"

"Can they watch that one?"

"Sure, go ahead. They're doing all right, though?"

"We're having a great time. Hope I didn't interrupt anything—"

"No, no, it's totally fine. Love you all."

"Have fun. See you in a few days!"

I hung up.

"Are they okay?" asked Pete.

"They're fine." I offered Pete a hand up. "Are we too protective? I mean, sometimes it seems like most kids are watching horror movies and playing realistic shoot-'em-ups before they're even out of grade school. We're still screening sitcoms from the nineties, for God's sake."

"Oh, no, Mrs. Monaco. There you go, breaking the rules again." He dusted the sand off himself. "I won't allow it. I'll have to feed you double-decker club sandwiches until you forget all about the children."

"Club sandwiches?" I punched his arm and grinned. "What children?"

"Last one to the shower's a rotten egg!"

We cleaned up and parked ourselves poolside with a pile of food until Luella, Rose, Oliver, Raphael, and Fisher arrived at the hotel. When we met them on the marina dock, it looked like a couples' cruise was about to depart—except for Fisher, who was very much the odd man out.

The flower in his leafy crown wasn't helping him blend in, either.

Rose corralled him against a railing. "So, where's the Eye? The real one, not the water sculpture."

"I do not know, Lady Fire Witch," he said, looking a bit nervous. "That is known only to my Mother."

"Leave the poor boy alone," Luella said.

"Boy? He's—"

I elbowed Rose before she blurted out Fisher's age.

"Not *that* young," she finished.

I introduced Pete to the other guys. Raphael looked sunny as usual in a bright Hawaiian shirt, whereas Oliver looked effortlessly cool in a sleek gray t-shirt and slacks. Rose had gone slightly off her Gothic look and veered toward the French Riviera in a black-and-white striped top and a pair of black shorts. Luella wouldn't have looked out of place in a summer window display at Chico's.

I had planned to pay for the rental and split the cost later, but Oliver intercepted me at the rental stand.

"Mrs. Millefleur requests that I pick up the tab on her behalf." He smoothly handed a credit card across the counter.

"Oh—" I fumbled with my purse. "I was going to—"

"She insists," he said, in a voice that brooked no argument.

Rose came up behind us. "Let her pay. It's the least she can do."

We boarded a sleek white boat called the *Tranquil Holiday*. There were enough seats for eight. A blue canopy provided some protection from the sun.

Oliver took the helm and piloted us out of the bay. The water slapped at the sides of the boat as we crossed the wakes of other vessels. Pelicans flew parallel to the waves, and the air smelled like brine. When we reached the open ocean, Oliver slowed the boat and called to Fisher. "Where to from here?"

Fisher had taken the seat closest to the bow. He gazed into the distance, toward the eastern horizon. "Do you know of the island that appears only at low tide?"

I nudged Pete. "Disappearing Island! We used to go there back in the day," I said to the others. "While the tide is low, you can beach there and spend a few hours on your own private island."

"Ooh," said Luella, with wide eyes.

Oliver reached into a cabinet in the helm and consulted a binder of laminated maps. "Disappearing Island it is."

"Look—dolphins!" said Raphael.

Sure enough, dolphins leaped from the blue water on both sides of the boat.

Rose's cat, Horatio, appeared with a pop and flash on her lap. He settled grumpily and lashed his tail. "I don't think he likes boating," said Rose.

A look of mild confusion flitted over Pete's face. "Who doesn't like boating?"

"Rose's familiar," I said. "He's on Rose's lap."

He peered at Rose, blinked, then gave a little shrug. "Can't see a thing."

"I think I can do something about that," she said. "Pepper, Luella, Raphael—summon your familiars." She cast Oliver a questioning glance. "Tea-and-crumpets? You in?"

"Of course."

Raphael called up his raccoon familiar, Princess. She clung to his Hawaiian shirt and peered around with shiny black eyes.

Luella's dog appeared in a blast of crosswind and jumped to the deck. Her tongue lolled like she was tasting the salt air.

I thought of Clove, and how she rode the sailboat with us on the second day of our trip. A scrabbling noise came from behind me, and Clove pulled herself up onto the stern. She shook off water, hopped across the deck, and took a perch on the bow, in front of Fisher.

Both of their noses pointed to the horizon.

Oliver returned the map binder to the cabinet and engaged the throttle. The boat surged smoothly forward.

"Oliver?" prompted Rose.

"Have I ever disappointed you, dear Rose?"

Her brow furrowed as her gaze swept the boat in search of a large bear.

I glanced around the boat, too. Then I looked over the starboard side.

Oliver's majestic bear familiar, Arthur, dashed across the water alongside the boat. His paws kicked up spray as he raced the dolphins.

Everyone but Pete and Oliver exclaimed as they caught sight of Arthur—Pete, of course, wasn't a witch and couldn't see a thing. "Do you need Pete to sit closer?" I asked Rose.

"I think I can do it from a little distance," she replied, angling herself toward Pete. "You want to see the familiars, right?'

"Yes, I do," he said.

"Look into my eyes."

Pete complied. His expression turned serious, like he was concentrating with his whole being.

Rose's eyes flashed silver, as they always did when she used her hypnosis magic. "See what I can see."

Pete's eyes flickered silver. He looked around the boat. When he caught sight of Clove, his eyes widened. "An otter! Pepper, is that *yours*?"

I smiled. "Pete, meet Clove the magical otter."

Pete's gaze took in Zephyr, Horatio, and Princess. "This is incredible!"

"Don't forget mine," said Oliver, dryly, but with a touch of pride.

Pete did a double take at the sight of the bear galloping across the water next to the leaping dolphins. Then he laughed. "This is unbelievable!"

The strain of the magic began to show on Rose's face. She closed her eyes and slumped against the seat. "Whew," she said.

"You all right?" Pete asked.

She nodded. "I'll be fine."

He put his arm around my shoulders and squeezed. "The Jimmy Stewart character had it all wrong. A witchy wife is a wonder."

I leaned my head to nuzzle his.

The engine purred and the sea spray fizzed rhythmically into the air as we flew across the water.

"Hey, Rose," said Raphael. "How's your sister doing these days?"

Rose straightened up. "Izzy?"

"Like, post-divorce-wise."

"It got a lot easier after Damon caved on the house."

"I was wondering if she found any resources in particular that were helpful."

"Books and therapy. I think there's a local support group, too. Why?"

A troubled expression flitted over his usually cheerful face. "There's this client at the legal aid clinic . . . she won't even come into the office, or give us any hard details. I think she's in hiding or something. Her ex-husband sounds like a pretty nasty guy."

"Nasty?" said Oliver.

"Some kind of CEO or something. Rich, powerful, and currently trying to ruin her life."

"What is a 'CEO'?" said Fisher.

"Someone who runs a large business," I said. "They're not all bad, but when they go bad, they have a lot of money and connections to go bad *with*."

Raphael nodded. "We're doing what we can over the phone, but I'm trying to think of anything else that might help."

Fisher regarded Raphael thoughtfully. "I should be glad to assist a lady in distress."

"Land ho!" cried Luella.

Princess scrambled to Raphael's shoulder and braced her paws on his head, presumably for a better look.

Disappearing Island lay before us.

16

The *Tranquil Holiday* slowed to idle speed. Disappearing Island stretched from north to south like a crescent moon lapped with crystal waves. Although the island was really nothing more than a glorified sandbar, its odd location and short-lived nature gave it a magical air.

Oliver's familiar waded ashore. The bear's thick fur dripped rivers of water.

Without warning, Fisher removed his shirt and vaulted over the side of the boat. He surfaced off the bow, paddling gracefully.

"I hope you're not expecting us to do that," called Rose.

"Do you not wish to, Lady Fire Witch? It is most pleasant."

Oliver smirked. "Go on, Rose. It's most pleasant."

"After you," she said.

I stood and dusted my hands. "Oliver has to stay with the boat. Raphael—will you stay, too? I don't want anyone to be alone."

Raphael attempted to wrangle Princess, who currently had two handfuls of his hair and was trying to steer him like he was a horse. "You bet."

"What about me?" said Pete.

"Do you want to stay?"

Pete cast a longing glance at the waves. "I will if you want me to."

"He should come," said Luella. "After all, you've worked in his office. It's about time he worked in yours."

"Call it 'Take Your Husband to Work Day,'" said Rose.

Pete was doing his best to make puppy dog eyes.

"Fine," I said. "You can come with us."

He made a triumphant gesture. "Hot dog."

"Fisher," I called. "Where do we go now?"

"I will open the water gate below the surface, Lady Pepper. We will descend from there."

"Will we have to swim?"

"No, lady." He disappeared beneath the surface.

I turned to Oliver. "Can you and Pete and Raphael shore anchor the boat? I need to talk to Luella and Rose for a minute." While the men set to work, I pulled my friends as far aside as I could in the small space. "I need to tell you something," I said quietly. "When I went surfing yesterday, a few of the Saltwater Folk popped up and tried to scare me off."

"Scare you off?" said Luella. "How?"

"Telling me to go away."

Luella and Rose traded apprehensive looks.

Rose raised an eyebrow. "You didn't want to mention this earlier?"

"I couldn't. We didn't see each other until today."

"We *were* on the dock earlier," Luella said.

I pulled my hair. "Okay, yes. I'm sorry! I could have mentioned it, but I didn't, because I thought you might bail—and if you want me to go by myself, I will—"

Luella put her hands on her hips. "Bail?"

Uh-oh. "I don't mean it like that—"

"Pepper, I love you, but if you keep implying that Rose and I aren't one-hundred-percent in on this, I will personally kick your butt from here to Miami."

Rose gave me a stern look and a firm nod.

They were right. Why was I pushing them away? Why had I assumed they wouldn't be there for me? I grabbed them both in a hug. "I'm an idiot."

Zephyr, Horatio, and Clove converged on us. Zephyr jumped from the seats to the deck and back again, while Horatio wound between our ankles, and Clove bounced around like a furry Slinky.

"There, there," said Luella. "We Ride-or-Die Witches always have each other's backs. Even when someone's being an idiot."

"*Especially* when someone's being an idiot," added Rose.

I released them. "Oh! One more thing. Don't worry—it's not bad. Well, not bad on my part, anyway. Remember how you told me Lenore disappeared from the spring that night?"

They nodded.

"I know how she did it."

They listened, their eyes growing wider as the implications sank in.

Luella shook her head. "Mrs. Millefleur has more secrets than a squirrel has acorns."

"Maybe we should ask Chuck where she hides them all," said Rose.

A splash drew our attention to Pete, Raphael, and Oliver. Clove hopped into the captain's chair for a better view.

Pete had jumped into the waist-deep water. He took the stern anchor fully ashore, near where Arthur sprawled on the sand like a seasoned sun-worshipper. Oliver dropped the bow anchor and trimmed up the engine. He and Raphael used the anchor lines to pull the boat into the proper position facing out to open water, then took in the slack. When they were finished, the boat rode the waves between the two anchored lines.

Pete waded out and rejoined us.

Off the port side, the sea began to churn—then it rose like a sideways, never-ending wave, swirling and foaming and sending off rainbow mist. Despite the turbulence, the water outside the immediate area didn't budge. When the mist blew away in the stiff breeze, sunlight revealed the sandy ocean floor in the center of the water arch.

"Nice tunnel," said Oliver.

Fisher emerged from the mouth of it. He bowed in our direction. "Lady witches, are you and your boon companion ready?"

Pete smiled and caught my gaze. "Boon companion."

"Come on, boon companion." I slapped him on the back. "Let's go."

We jumped in from the stern of the boat. The sand swirled under my feet as I waded through the waist-deep water over to Fisher's tunnel. Clove shot through the water ahead of me.

Horatio rode on Rose's shoulders, and Zephyr dashed back and forth across the water as if she were too impatient to walk at a human's pace.

The water magically stopped at the entrance to the tunnel as if it were held back by an invisible fence. We emerged onto the cool, wet sand where the sea had been rolled back.

Fisher took the lead. I followed him with Clove at my heels. Luella and Zephyr walked behind me, followed by Rose and Horatio, then Pete.

The seabed sloped down from the island. Tiny white crabs scuttled out of the watery walls and crossed our path. We descended further into the tunnel, the sunlight fading with each step. The air reminded me of being buried in the sand, with the beach so close to my nose that I couldn't help inhaling the scent.

When we reached a point where I was sure I'd have to start feeling my way forward in the dark, Fisher ignited the water with glowing light, just as he'd done in the underground river caves—except these lights were blue, not green.

The tunnel ended at an open area with a planetarium-sized water dome serving as the ceiling and the walls. The height of the dome made it such that some sunlight filtered down to the seafloor, but a lot of the illumination still came from the glowing swirls of blue lights on the watery walls. Shells of all sizes studded the sand like discarded toys.

"Where is everyone?" I said.

"Pepper—" said Pete.

"I mean, I wasn't expecting a welcoming committee, but at least the Sweetwater Folk had the decency to show up—"

"Pepper. Look at the walls."

"Walls?" The blue glare stopped me from seeing clearly, at first. Then, I focused beyond the lights, beyond whatever invisible force was holding back the ocean.

Large shadows moved. Metallic scales caught the blue light and sent flashes of illumination winking through the barrier.

"Oh," I said. "They're here. They're just not *in* here."

Clove hopped assertively over to the far edge of the dome and nudged her nose into the water.

The water rippled. The lights wavered.

Clove backpedaled.

A surfboard carrying a human figure shot out of the water and flew through the air.

It hit the sand with a thump and skidded to a stop in front of us. The rider hopped off and ran her hands through her short, tousled hair. Water dripped from a thick seaweed skirt and a more sparse seaweed stole.

The woman casually scooped up Clove, who seemed too surprised or curious to wiggle away. She hefted the otter like a baby, under the arms, as if to see how much she weighed. She turned her this way and that. "A fine wee lass," she said. She set Clove down.

Clove blinked, then sat down and began grooming her face with her paws.

Fisher folded into a bow. "My Mother," he said, with formal grace, "I present the youngest witch, her boon companion, and her fellow young witches."

The Saltwater Queen—it had to be her, there was no one else Fisher would have addressed like that—swaggered forward. Up close, her dark hair was shot through with gray, and decorated with dozens of tiny shells that made a rustling sound when she shook her head. "You've been hanging around the river Folk too much, my boy."

Fisher straightened. "It is as you say, my Mother."

She patted his cheek with obvious affection.

"Where is Lenore?" said Rose. Horatio hissed, and fire danced over Rose's fingertips.

The queen cast her an amused look. "Calm down, witch. Can't you see where you are?" Her gaze swept the watery surroundings. "Your fire powers wouldn't hold up here. You might try relaxing for a minute or two before you start making demands."

"No offense, your Majesty," said Luella, with a quelling glance at Rose, "but we want to make sure our, uh . . . *friend* is okay."

"Especially after you sent your people after me yesterday," I added.

Pete shot me a look of alarm.

I winced. I hadn't gotten around to mentioning that incident to him yet.

The Saltwater Queen took a seat on the surfboard and leaned back, which showed off the abstract blue tattoos on her arms. "Ah, they were just having a laugh." The charming smile that accompanied this could have been genuine—or vaguely threatening.

Meanwhile, Zephyr wandered over and sniffed around the surfboard.

The queen patted the dog's head and ruffled her ears. "I tell you what—I'll make it up to you."

"No, really, that's not necessary. We just want to know where—"

She put her fingers to her lips and whistled.

17

The lower reaches of the water dome splashed and sprayed as a horde of Saltwater Folk poured in, their tails instantly transforming into legs as they came through. They wore seaweed like the queen, and had all lengths of salt-stiffened hair. Some had blue-stained lips; others, blue-stained nails. Several ran to the queen's surfboard and lifted it like it was a litter.

The Saltwater Queen threw her head back and laughed. She climbed to a standing position on the board, then completed a perfect forward flip to land in the middle of the crowd.

A group of Saltwater Folk ran to the dome's edge and received a delivery of fish—still flopping—handed over by the merpeople swimming outside the dome. The queen's surfboard was laid down, and a wicked-looking knife wielded, and shining slices of fresh fish were handed to us on delicate shell plates.

I loved a good California roll, but had never quite gotten up to speed on the raw stuff.

Pete, on the other hand, was already stuffing the slices in his mouth with the air of a man who has died and gone to sushi heaven. "You know how much this would cost at a restaurant?"

Luella—always the polite guest—made a show of taking a bite. She rubbed her belly. "Yum, yum." Then she surreptitiously hid the shell behind her back and let Zephyr have the rest.

Horatio sniffed at Rose's sushi until Rose started feeding him tidbits.

Another crowd of Saltwater Folk had brought in makeshift drums, pipes, and rattles. They struck up a song that veered between a sea shanty, an Irish jig, and a punk rock anthem. The half-sung, half-shouted lyrics were mostly about life in the ocean—with an interesting assortment of swear words thrown in straight out of the merchant marines.

Pete indicated my shell plate. "Are you going to finish that?"

I wordlessly handed him the shell.

More Saltwater Folk poured in from outside the dome and began to gyrate wildly to the music. Occasionally, the merpeople at the surfboard-turned-cutting-board flung slices of fish into the crowd, which were snatched out of the air with shouts of triumph by the catchers.

"Fisher!" called the queen. "Join the dance!"

Fisher dutifully hurried forward into the surging mass of Saltwater Folk. While his mother danced wildly at the center of a circle of revelers, he hovered on the edge and made awkward movements to the beat.

"They do know how to throw a party," said Luella.

"Like a mosh pit at the bottom of the sea," said Rose.

Pete polished off the last piece of fish and gave the empty shells a forlorn look.

I threw my hands up. "How am I supposed to be negotiating when all they're doing is boogieing down?"

"Reminds me of that bonfire party you took me to on our first date," said Pete.

"That was probably the last time we danced like that." I grabbed Pete's hand. "Come on."

"Are you sure we should—"

"Pretend you're twenty!" I pulled him along into the center of the impromptu dance floor. We would dance our way to the queen, and I would come up with something genius on the way.

Pete kicked it off with a little Mashed Potato.

I countered with the Twist.

He segued into the Watusi while I added the Swim.

I caught the Saltwater Queen looking at us with a strange expression on her face—a mix of approval and something melancholy, as if it made her happy and sad to watch us.

Why?

The Sweetwater Queen's words came back, drifting through the clamor like an undercurrent: *I remember the bay, where once we met in peace . . .*

Maybe the Sweetwater Queen wasn't the only one who remembered a lost love.

Negotiating with the Sweetwater Queen and with Mrs. Millefleur turned into a confrontation. This called for a more subtle approach.

I could do subtle.

I'd take the Saltwater Queen for a little walk down memory lane.

Soften her up.

I mentally patted myself on the back, then gestured to Pete to move closer to the queen. He nodded and Watusi-ed in her direction. I kept up the Swim and followed. Since it wasn't exactly a partnered dance—the Saltwater Folk free-flowed in and out of little groups—we were able to sidle up next to her.

The shells in her hair whipped and clashed as she thrash-danced to the rhythm of the drums.

"Your Majesty—"

She dialed back the fierce movements just enough to meet my gaze.

"I have a message for you."

"Aye, lass? Say on."

It took a little more volume to be heard over the noise. "The Sweetwater Queen wants you to remember the bay where you met in peace."

The Saltwater Queen stopped dancing.

As if the musicians shared one mind with the queen, the music stopped, too. The dancers stilled.

Blue light sparked in the queen's eyes. "What did you say?"

The Saltwater Folk backed slowly away from Pete, the queen, and me.

Oops. What *had* I said? "I, uh—I was just saying that she seems to remember it fondly, and—"

The queen whirled around to her people. "'Fondly,' she says! The stuck-up underground princess remembers it *fondly*!"

The Saltwater Folk looked unsure of how to react. Some laughed. Some jeered.

The queen seized her surfboard and flung it with super-human strength.

Merpeople dove out of the way to avoid being flattened. "I'll show her fondly!"

Fisher ran toward her. "Mother, no!"

The queen ignored him and dropped to her knees. Balls of blue light appeared in her hands. Fisher bounced off the crackling blue force field surrounding her and staggered back.

The ground rumbled. The water dome shook.

The Saltwater Folk ran for the walls and dove through, their legs transforming into tails as they hit the water and disappeared into the sea.

Now it was just the queen, Fisher, the four of us, and the familiars.

I didn't know what I'd done, but I had to fix it. "Your Majesty—"

The queen closed her eyes and howled. Unlike the Sweetwater Queen, water didn't pour from her mouth and hands. Instead, an answering howl vibrated the water dome.

The tunnel to the surface collapsed, sealing us inside the dome. A long, black shadow circled outside.

Water dripped on my face like cold, salty tears. The dome was leaking.

The sea wanted back in.

Clove clung to my leg. What would happen if the dome fell on our heads?

Pete looked at me with fear in his eyes—and, worst of all, *hope*. Like he thought I'd know what to do.

In my rush to bring back the good feelings between the Saltwater and Sweetwater Queens, I'd forgotten what paves memory lane: all the little things that pile up day after day, like Legos, that you're only able to ignore until you step on one and it drives right into your heel. Yelling only feels good until the anger fades and everything is still the same.

It didn't matter whether the relationship was between mermaid queens, an accountant and a dentist, or siblings. The time would come when you had to face what you ignored.

You had to clean up the damn Legos.

I reached with my magic, palms facing the roof of the dome in a mirror of the queen's open hands—except instead of roiling the water, I smoothed it. Just like the baby blanket back at home.

The weight pressed down, but I held strong. "Hush," I said. "Hush. It's okay." The dome shimmered with light as my silver magic swirled through the Saltwater Folk's blue magic. To my surprise, the two magics wove together, then tightened like a knot.

The dripping stopped.

And then a monstrous horse head with fins broke through the far wall of the dome.

18

Two massive crab legs, a sturdy horse's body, and a dragon-like tail followed the silver-finned horse face through the wall. The horse-crab-dragon thing opened its mouth and roared, drumming its crab legs on the sand while whipping the fishy tip of its tail through the air.

"Oh, crap," I said.

All of us backpedaled away—except for the queen, who remained kneeling and silent on the ground, her back to the monster.

The thing moved like a cross between a rototiller and a sidewinder, its forelegs cycling forward while its body looped and pushed off from behind.

"Fisher," said Rose, without taking her eyes off the sea monster, "what is that thing?"

"It is the Hipocampo. The queen's war horse."

"Why is she still sitting there with her eyes closed?"

"She is at one with the sea. It takes great concentration to summon the Hipocampo. She must withdraw from it slowly, lest she injure herself."

"And who's in charge of Mr. Hipocampo right now?" said Luella.

Fisher shook his head slowly.

"Oh, excellent," said Pete.

"Quiet," said Rose. "Everyone be quiet."

Her eyes flashed silver.

The great beast blinked and cocked its head. Then its eyes flickered silver, too. It shied back, flicked its tail, and tossed its head like it was throwing off a bridle.

"Easy, there." Rose took a step forward.

It made a grunting noise and batted at its own face with one leg, then skittered back.

She extended her hand. "Down, boy."

The Hipocampo crouched, framing its horse head between its crab forelegs. Its tail popped up in a curve over its body, and wagged like a friendly dog.

"That's better. Let's have a look at you."

Luella started forward. "Rose, be careful—"

"I got this." She stepped to the side of the Hipocampo and stroked its neck. "There, now. Isn't that nicer than howling and growling? Good boy."

The Hipocampo whinnied and waved its foreleg, causing Rose to dance back.

"Watch it," I said. "If you got killed by a horse's crab leg, I'd never forgive myself."

Rose gave a faint smile. She eased up to the Hipocampo again. "What's the matter? Are you hurt?" Her eyes flickered silver again as she placed her hand on the Hipocampo's head. She glided her hand down the creature's long nose, then lifted its lip and peered at its gums. "There's something wrong with its tooth."

The Saltwater Queen, who had been sitting motionless the whole time, finally stirred. The blue magic in her hands crackled and fizzed out. She opened her eyes.

Fisher hurried to her side.

Seeing as how Rose had the Hipocampo situation in hand, I stalked across the sand to confront the queen. "What's the big idea, then? Throw a fit and put everyone in danger just because you got reminded of your lost love?"

Fisher's mouth fell open.

"Uh, Pepper," said Luella.

"Don't bother," said Pete. "She's not going to stop once she gets going."

The Saltwater Queen sprang to her feet and pushed past me, heading toward the Hipocampo. "Fisher, we ride to defeat the Sweetwater Folk once and for all. It is long past time when the sea should retake its rightful place."

"Mother, no!"

She rounded on him. "What are you, then? Are you her son, or mine?"

"I cannot choose between you—not now, not ever."

I stepped between them, putting Fisher behind me. "You're a real piece of work, you know that? And the third person I've talked to this week who could benefit from some therapy."

"What is 'therapy'?" said Fisher.

"A way to stop doing the same stupid things over and over again."

"I would try this 'therapy,'" he said. "Perhaps my Mothers could come with me."

"Away with you, water witch," said the queen. "There's nothing left to negotiate."

"There damn well is. You're not going anywhere on this thing, not if you have a heart somewhere under all that seaweed."

Pete joined Rose and peered at the Hipocampo's exposed teeth. "Yeah, that needs to be fixed before it gets infected."

The Saltwater Queen looked at the Hipocampo. "What does he mean?"

"It has a bad tooth," said Pete. "A cavity. In my professional opinion, the tooth needs to be repaired before it gets worse. I'm going to need a few things first, though." He ticked items off on his fingers. "My drill, some filling materials, lidocaine—and how are we going to sedate it?" His gaze traveled from the creature's horse head to its fish tail. "It's the size of a Clydesdale."

All eyes went to the queen. Even Clove, Zephyr, and Horatio stared at her.

She shifted uncomfortably. "I wasn't going to hurt it—"

Rose patted the knobbly carapace of the Hipocampo's closest front leg. "You didn't seem particularly concerned about it. You were going to ride off without a second thought."

"Poor Hipocampo," added Luella.

I stepped in and gently angled the Hipocampo's horse face toward the queen. "Look at this sweet face," I said. "How can you make it go to war?"

The Hipocampo rolled its eyes and let out a pitiful whinny. For a giant horse-crab-dragon monster, it did a pretty good job of playing for sympathy.

"All right!" said the queen. Her face softened. "What do you want me to do? I don't have any of those things."

"Then this is your lucky day, because my husband is a professional tooth-fixer."

The Saltwater Queen approached the Hipocampo. It laid its head over her shoulder, and she smoothed her hands over its neck. "I'll not have my loyal friend suffer. Tell me what you wish in return."

"First, I want to see the woman you took from the spring. Lenore."

"Done."

"Second, you and the Sweetwater Queen need to work it out, not go to war."

The queen bowed her head, placing her forehead against the Hipocampo's neck. "Ah, water witch. You don't know what you're asking."

"I do, though. You're not the only person in here who's been married for a long time. You need to talk to each other instead of passive-aggressively stealing stuff—"

"People," said Rose.

"—or dropping backhanded hints about how good the old days used to be. Someone has to take a risk. Maybe you'll make up. Or maybe you'll end things like adults, I don't know. But anything's got to be better than this."

"The Lady Pepper is wise, Mother," said Fisher.

"And my husband, who's a bonafide tooth repairman, will fix up your Hipocampo as good as new."

Pete stood tall, possibly in an attempt to look more dentist-like. His soaked casual outfit didn't offer reassurance quite as well as his usual crisp white coat.

The Saltwater Queen patted the Hipocampo's nose. "What do you think, my friend? Is it a fair bargain?"

The Hipocampo whickered, then sneezed a spray of saltwater on all of us.

"First sulfur, now this," said Rose, flicking her hands in disgust.

"I accept," said the queen. "Tooth Repair Man, you will help my Hipocampo."

Fisher reopened the water tunnel and took Pete, Luella, and Rose topside.

The Saltwater Queen released the Hipocampo and slowly collapsed the water dome until it was as small as a backyard greenhouse, just big enough to hold the two of us comfortably.

Clove poked at the wall, making sparks of light flit across the surface.

"Are you sure my friends can't come with me to see Lenore?"

The queen removed one of the shells from her hair. "This is only for you." She tugged a lock of my hair free and knotted the shell into it with a bit of cord.

A funny feeling trickled down from my scalp like someone had poured cold water over my head. Blue sparks tumbled down my shoulders to my hips and legs, finally fanning out and swirling around my feet. "What are you doing to me?"

"You wanted to see Lenore, didn't you?"

"Well, yeah—"

"How else did you think you were going to swim there?"

"Swim there? But I can't breathe underwater . . ."

The queen flicked the shell in my hair. "See for yourself." With a mighty shove—she was far stronger than she looked—the queen knocked me through the dome wall and into the water.

The second I passed the barrier I lost my footing. I flailed to right myself and get back into the dome of air, but I could hardly tell which way was up, thanks to the cloud of bubbles that surrounded me.

How long could I hold my breath?

And why weren't my feet kicking properly? My shorts seemed to be caught—

Oh.

I didn't have feet.

I had a fin.

I didn't have legs.

I had a tail.

My shorts and underwear had gotten hung up around where my thighs should have been. I wriggled out of them, abandoning them in the swirling water, and pushed off as hard as I could. The motion sent me surging toward the sunlight and oxygen as the instinct to inhale got stronger.

Closer, closer . . . until I couldn't hold it anymore. My mouth popped open and my lungs sucked in—
Air.

19

Never had fishy, salty air tasted so good. I stopped swimming for the surface when I realized the Saltwater Queen hadn't been lying—I could breathe as easily as I could above the water.

I hovered, taking deep breaths and getting my bearings. There was the miniature water dome below. To the west, the shadow of the rental boat. To the east, a dark dropoff. And all around the silhouettes and reflective scales of fish.

Clove swam up from below and barrel-rolled gleefully past.

I brought my tail forward and gave it an experimental flap. The scales matched the pearl on my necklace, all black and green with hints of rainbow, stopping a few inches above where my C-section scar would be.

I pushed away a few free-floating curls that kept wandering in front of my face and swam toward the water dome.

My t-shirt and bra weren't built for swimming, but I wasn't exactly ready to go full French sunbather.

When I was halfway there, the queen emerged from the dome in a swirling cloud of silt and bubbles. When she was clear of it, the dome itself collapsed with a fizzing blast of bubbles. She surged upward out of the disturbance and joined me at my depth.

I made a thumbs-up motion toward the surface, hoping she'd get the hint so we could talk.

She shook her head slowly and deliberately, making her short hair spin outward like an automatic car wash brush. *No need, water witch.*

The words arrived in my head as if I were wearing headphones.

Cool, I thought.

The current pushed away the queen's seaweed mantle.

Oof. Mardi Gras under the sea!

I pulled off my shirt and held it toward the Saltwater Queen with a meaningful look. The *Monaco Family Dental* logo billowed in the water.

The Saltwater Queen turned a somersault with a laugh that came out in bubbles. *Human modesty.* She rolled her eyes but took the shirt. After detaching her mantle, she tugged on the t-shirt inside out and backwards. It looked strange above her deep blue tail. She plucked at it, then swam toward the dark drop-off.

Clove and I followed. I was so used to swimming with my arms that it was hard not to use them, even though I didn't need to. Instead I was getting an intense abdominal workout from the up and down whip-like motion of my shiny new tail.

We crossed a ridge on the seabed and dove deeper.

Beneath the edge of the ridge, an air bubble the size of a hot air balloon covered the mouth of a cave.

The queen pivoted to face it, surged forward, and plunged through the bubble.

I hesitated. If my legs didn't show up when I passed through, I'd end up doing a painful belly flop. I swam to the bubble and tentatively stuck my arm through.

Someone inside grabbed it and pulled.

I was through the barrier before I could even register what was happening, stumbling and then landing sideways on the cave floor. The walls glowed blue with the same sea magic as the tunnel and the big dome.

At least my legs were back—but why did my butt feel so cold?

"My pants!" I curled my legs up to preserve at least a tiny bit of modesty.

The queen—wearing my t-shirt, with her seaweed skirt back in place after her own mermaid-to-human transformation—doubled over laughing.

A warm, husky laugh echoed behind her. An older woman stepped forward and gave me a slow clap. Her hair was neatly bundled up in a braid crown, and she had a shock of bright white hair rising from her hairline.

Lenore.

I scowled. "Could you stop laughing for a second and maybe find something for me to cover up with?"

They laughed so hard they had to hold each other up.

Lenore wiped the corners of her eyes. She retreated to a corner of the cave, her shoulders still shaking, and picked up a blanket. She tossed it to me. "So you're the famous Pepper."

I wrapped myself up. "And you're the famous—or should I say *infamous*—Lenore."

Lenore looked less than offended. "Salty, could you give us a moment?"

"You're not afraid to be alone with her?" The Saltwater Queen gave me an amused once-over.

Lenore snorted. "She's harmless."

"Harmless?" I drew myself up as much as I could while sitting on the floor and not wearing pants.

The queen dove through the bubble wall, leaving me alone with Lenore, thief of magic, sister of Mrs. Millefleur, and all-around pain in the ass.

Up close, she didn't seem as intimidating as I thought she'd be. Especially in this weirdly cozy, Jessica-Fletcher-under-the-sea cave complete with salvaged chairs, a tiny dining table with a blue-and-white checkered tablecloth, and a mismatched collection of teacups on the wall. Toward the back, I spied a neatly made cot topped with frilly throw pillows.

I had come to rescue her. Fighting with her seemed like a waste of energy. Besides, I was kind of tired, and it felt good to take a breather. I rolled my ankles and flexed my feet, happy to see my toes again. "*Salty*? Really?"

She dragged over a chair and sat. "We're friends." She shifted, revealing a corded necklace that disappeared into her shirt. Her leggings and puffy vest must have been keeping her warm, making me wish I had something more than a bra and blanket.

"How did you make friends with the mermaids who kidnapped you?"

"They're suckers for a good story. And I had a whopper."

"The one about how you tried to steal your sister's magic and my friend's magic?"

"Ah, but *why*?"

"Your employer stole your retirement fund and you lost everything."

"And what would you do if that happened to you?"

"Probably not steal other people's magic."

Lenore made a derisive noise. "Everyone thinks they wouldn't do something like that—until they do. What if it was a choice between living in a cardboard box and sponging off your grown children?"

"You have *kids*?"

She fished in her vest pocket, then pulled out and brandished a small flip phone. "Gotta call my son every night or he gets antsy."

"But . . . you could just go *home*. Why stay in a cold undersea cave?"

She settled back in the chair. "I stole from a big museum. I managed to antagonize my sister and your friend pretty well, too. Why should I deal with everyone coming after me when I can stay someplace quiet? Besides, home is boring. This place is interesting."

"You're old enough to retire! Live the dream!"

Lenore smirked. "And do what? Play shuffleboard? Fat chance. I was sick of being the invisible woman."

"What do you mean, 'the invisible woman'?"

"When you go shopping and no one asks if you need help. When people at work ask for ideas and ignore yours. When doctors don't listen to a damn word you say." She gestured with both hands, as if that would help me get it. "Invisible."

I didn't want to admit I knew exactly what she was talking about.

Lenore leaned forward. A silver key tumbled out of her v-neck and swung free on the cord. She followed my gaze to the Key, and a half-smile lifted one corner of her lips. "I won't be invisible unless it's on *my* terms."

Oh, I was going to wipe that smug look right off her face. "I bet you don't know where it came from, do you? That key?"

Her eyes narrowed.

Ha! Score one for me. "Do you want to know?"

"What'll it cost me?"

"Come back with me. Talk to your sister."

"My sister can rot."

"Wouldn't it be nice not to have to live on the run anymore? Isn't your son going to get worried?"

She laughed. "Don't try to manipulate me, kiddo." She stood and walked to the far corner of the cave, where she picked up a bag. She rifled through it, pulled out a wrinkled sticky note, and squinted as she read it aloud. "Hildegarde Millefleur, 1153 Atlantic Avenue, Sparkle Beach, Florida."

"So you know where your own sister lives. Is that supposed to be some kind of threat?"

"If I wanted to make a threat it would be a hell of a lot better than something I could pull out of a phone book. No, this is a copy of something I found somewhere else. Someone has my sister's name and address, and some other dangerous information you might be interested in. Someone nasty. And if you or your friends try to pull any funny business while I'm topside, you won't find out who."

I scrambled up, blanket and all, and lunged for the sticky note.

She didn't even try to dodge.

I snatched it and furiously examined it, front and back. "There's nothing else on here."

Lenore tapped her temple. "There doesn't need to be." She held out her hand.

I hesitated—then slapped the note into it. What was I going to do with a sticky note with Mrs. Millefleur's address on it? Nothing.

Lenore's smile was more grim than triumphant as she pulled a spotted shell from another pocket and held it to her ear like a phone. "Better call Salty."

20

"Is there any way I can stay dry this time?" I asked the Saltwater Queen. "If I turn mermaid again, I'll soak my coverup, and I don't love the idea of returning to the surface in a wet bra and blanket."

"You can go like me," said Lenore. "She puts me in a bubble and pulls me along. Jump through and you'll see."

Salty untied the mermaid transformation shell from my hair. "Piece of cake, lass." She stepped back, making way for Lenore.

Lenore hopped through the bubble barrier like she'd been doing it all her life.

Although I'd been a repeat witness to the Saltwater Folk's magic, I still hesitated to jump through the bubble into the cold, deep sea—but I wasn't about to be shown up by Lenore. I held my borrowed blanket tightly and jumped.

A body-sized air bubble enveloped me like a soft submarine pod. When I moved my free arm outward, the bubble stretched like saltwater taffy. I took a few breaths and my bubble began to float upward.

It was hard to see anything outside the bubble thanks to the distortion of the water and the little bubbles that fizzed off the surface of the big one. I could make out a second bubble nearby, which must have been Lenore, but the reflective surface made it difficult to see inside of it.

The Saltwater Queen appeared between us, and the bubble tilted forward, putting me in a prone position. It moved with a motion not too different from a Disney monorail sliding along its track. I summoned Clove to keep me company, and she snuggled next to me with her whiskers twitching.

"This is fun," I said to her, "but I kind of wish Luella and Rose had gotten to come along."

Clove rested her head on my shoulder.

"They would probably like being mermaids. We could go swimming in the ocean, or in one of the springs—don't wrinkle your nose at me, I don't mean the stinky green one—or maybe just in the pool at home."

She made a soft squeaking noise.

"I know I have a lot of responsibilities, but maybe there'll be time to have fun later. After I deal with Lenore, and Mrs. Millefleur, and Salty, and . . . oh, I know the *perfect* nickname for the Sweetwater Queen!"

The air bubble slowed and drifted upward again. My weight shifted to my feet.

"I think we're here." I secured my blanket with one hand and wrapped the other arm around Clove.

The bubble rose like an elevator. The top broke the surface and disappeared. The boat appeared to my left, but no one appeared to be on board. Lenore popped up on my right. The half-bubbles sped on shore like little motorboats and dissolved completely when the water became knee-height.

Clove hopped down and dashed through the surf.

The earth witches had been busy. A gigantic sand castle rose on the island—a real sand castle, not a concrete imitation like the one on the hotel minigolf course.

We splashed onshore.

Luella and Rose hurried from the front of the sand castle to the water's edge.

Rose stopped when she spotted Lenore. "You."

Lenore raised her hands. "Chill out. I'm not here to fight."

"Like hell," said Rose. She ignited balls of silver fire in both hands.

I held one hand up while holding my modesty blanket in place with the other. "Rose! Be cool."

The flames shrank but didn't disappear.

I turned to Lenore. "And don't antagonize my friend."

"I didn't antagonize her—"

"Telling Rose to 'chill out' is the number one way to antagonize her."

"You did it, too," grumbled Lenore.

Oliver and Raphael emerged from behind the giant sand castle.

Oliver froze. "You."

Rose smirked. "That's what I said."

Sand boiled around Lenore's feet. Oliver's magic sent it crawling upward over itself like it would swallow Lenore whole. She stumbled backward and landed on her backside. Sand engulfed her feet and started covering her legs.

"Stop it!" I said. "I know we're all mad at her. But this was a rescue, remember? I'm supposed to bring her back to her sister."

"Pepper's right," said Luella. "No flaming and no burying people in sand until Mrs. Millefleur's had her say."

The sand retreated—it looked almost reluctant—and Rose extinguished her fire.

I gave Lenore a stern look. "Don't think I won't be the first to blast you if you try anything stupid."

Lenore didn't appear to be listening. Instead, she was peering at my husband, who had followed Oliver and Raphael out from behind the sand castle. She waved cheerfully. "Hi, Dr. Monaco!"

Pete blinked. "Gold coin lady?"

I looked back and forth between the two of them. "*This* is the gold coin lady?"

Lenore shrugged. "I was short on cash. No ATMs under the sea." She stood and brushed off sand.

Sure. Mrs. Millefleur's sister had been getting dental work from my husband. That made at least as much sense as underground mermaids and horse-crab-dragon monsters.

"By the way," said Pete, eyeing the blanket, "what happened to your clothes?"

"It's a long story. Where's Fisher?"

"He said it was too dry up here, so he went swimming."

"Tide's coming in. We better get off this island before it disappears."

We waded out to the *Tranquil Holiday*. Lenore took the seat closest to the bow. Rose sat as far away from her as possible. Oliver took the helm, and the rest of us took the remaining seats.

I cupped my hands around my mouth. "Fisher! Let's go!"

He popped up off the side of the boat. "Must we, Lady Pepper? I was only beginning to enjoy the water." He swam effortlessly to the stern and climbed the stairs. His shirt remained on the seat—but he must have stayed in human form for his swim, because he still had Pete's shorts on.

With Fisher in the last available seat, we headed toward the bay. No one seemed to want to talk around Lenore, so the ride was quieter than it was on the way out.

When we reached the marina, a female figure wearing a navy blue skirt and blazer topped with a broad-brimmed hat in the same color stood on the dock.

"Oh, hell," said Lenore. "You didn't tell me I'd have to see her *right now.*"

The woman on the dock raised her head, lifting the wide brim of her hat and revealing her face.

Mrs. Millefleur gave the *Tranquil Holiday* a look like it had offended her personally. "All this trouble to retrieve you," she said. "I don't know why I bother."

Lenore stood up like she might jump out of the boat to confront her sister. "Like you're some kind of good Samaritan. Give me a break."

"If I'd had a choice, I'd have left you right where you were. You should thank Pepper for convincing me otherwise."

"You should thank your sister for sending you that key," I said to Lenore.

Dead silence.

"You're lying," said Lenore.

A half-smile lifted the corner of Mrs. Millefleur's lips. "Is she?"

Lenore climbed down to the dock.

The rest of us scrambled to one side of the boat to watch, making it tip slightly.

"I bought this key online. You had nothing to do with it."

"You poor, deluded thing. The auction listing? The one you just couldn't pass up? I created it. I sold you the Key."

"That's ridiculous. How would you have known I would look for a key?"

Mrs. Millefleur's expression turned smug.

"You *witch*," said Lenore. "You hypnotized me."

Luella nudged me. "Maybe we should intervene before they take a swing at each other."

"Definitely don't intervene," said Rose.

"It's not like you would have listened to me otherwise," said Mrs. Millefleur.

"That doesn't give you the right to go messing around in my head!"

People down the dock turned to look at the two of them.

"We're going to get our cover blown if they don't shut up." I hustled down to the dock and stepped between them. "Break it up, you two. You can't do this at full volume in the middle of a marina."

"How about I throw her in and be done with it?" said Lenore.

"Quiet. Nobody's throwing anyone in. Pete," I called. "What time is our spa appointment?"

Pete, who had followed me down, checked his watch. "Twenty minutes."

"You two are *not* ruining my romantic couple's massage."

Mrs. Millefleur looked me up and down. "You're already dressed for it. Or should I say *un*-dressed for it?"

"What is it with you two?" I raised my eyes to the sky. "The best punishment would be to lock you in a room together and let you murder each other. I don't have time for this."

Fisher came up behind us. "Your pardon, Lady Pepper. I could not help but overhear."

"Who is this guy, anyway?" said Lenore.

"Never you mind," said Mrs. Millefleur.

Fisher cleared his throat and continued. "I understand that you plan to have a massage, do you not? For the relief of your aches and pains?"

"Where's he going with this?" murmured Pete.

I motioned him to silence.

"I could not help but notice that the elder Lady Fire Witch wears most uncomfortable looking shoes—"

"*Elder* fire witch?" sputtered Mrs. Millefleur.

"And that her sister, the Lady Lenore, has been long in a place that is not always rich in human comforts. Is it not so?"

"It *is* so," I said, nodding vehemently.

"Then mayhap it is best for their comfort to be treated as you will be treated, Lady Pepper. It may improve the sorest temper."

I clapped my hand on his very firm bicep. "Fisher, you're a genius. I'm sure they can fit in two more people."

"For what?" said Lenore.

"For a nice, relaxing massage. Both of you can calm down and discuss things with cooler heads." I retucked my blanket cover-up—boy, was I looking forward to that nice, fluffy spa robe—then I turned to the rest of my friends, who had joined us on the dock. "Anybody got plans for tonight?" I gave them what I hoped was my most convincing smile. "Wanna wrestle a sea monster into a dentist's office?"

21

"You don't understand," said Mrs. Millefleur, who had insisted on holding on to Lenore all the way to the spa. "If I let go, she could disappear in an instant."

I inhaled the eucalyptus-scented air and tried to focus on the soft tones of the soothing spa music. "Then hold hands during the massage."

"I'm not doing that," said Lenore. "This has been embarrassing enough without holding hands like I'm a little kid. What if I have to use the bathroom?"

I turned a magazine page like I couldn't be bothered. "Either you give up the Key or you keep holding her hand. Your choice." I'd never realized how much my experience with settling the boys' fights would come in handy.

"I'm not giving it to *her*."

I held out my hand without looking up.

"Are you crazy? That's my escape route."

I shut the magazine and met her gaze. "You're with us now, whether you like it or not. If we feel you're in danger, we'll help you. Up to and including with the Key. But you're going to have to trust someone, and if it's not going to be your sister, it might as well be me. I'm the harmless one, remember?"

Lenore's head tilted back as she regarded me. "Now I'm not so sure." She hesitated. Then she slowly drew the Key up from under her shirt. She pulled the necklace over her head. She held the cord in her fist, the Key dangling, while she gave me another searching look. After a pause, she presented the necklace to me. "Don't let it touch your skin. And if you do, don't even think about entering another world. It's very sensitive."

"That's like saying don't think about pink manatees." I took the cord and held it at arm's length. Where would I put it during the massage?

Lenore grabbed a lavender sachet from the nearest side table. She dumped the contents in a small trash can and passed me the empty muslin bag. "Here. Put this around it. It'll keep the Key off your skin. If you end up in the shadows by accident, picture the real world to return."

I put the cord around my neck, taking care to let the Key rest on the thick white collar of the spa bathrobe. Then I slipped the Key into the bag and pulled the drawstrings tight.

A spa attendant appeared with a clipboard. "We are ready to begin your Relax Package."

Pete tossed the magazine he'd been flipping through onto the coffee table. "That's us."

We split up, Mrs. Millefleur and Lenore to one treatment room, Pete and I to the other.

Inside the darkened room, the mood lighting glinted on Pete's glasses. He removed them and set them aside. "What with it being so busy and all, we haven't really had time to talk."

No talk that starts like that could possibly be a fun conversation. I unbelted the robe and let it fall, hoping the view would put a quick end to having to "talk."

No dice. He had turned away. "What happened when you went surfing?"

"It was no big deal."

"If it was no big deal, then why couldn't you tell me about it?"

I hated how calm he sounded. So freaking reasonable. I hurried onto the massage table and pulled the sheet over myself. "Some of the Saltwater Folk told me to go away, okay? What else do you want to know?"

The sound of fabric hitting a chair indicated he'd taken off his bathrobe, too. The massage table creaked as he climbed on, followed by a whoosh of air as he freed the top sheet and draped himself. "Why didn't you tell me?"

"Don't you trust my judgment?"

A pause. Then, quietly: "Don't you trust me enough not to keep secrets?"

Someone knocked at the door, thank God.

"Come in," I called.

Two spa attendants entered the treatment room. "Would you like an aromatherapy oil?" one of them asked.

"Yes," I said. "Whichever one is for *relaxation*." I emphasized the last word in hopes that Peter would get the message and knock off the serious talk.

The scent of lavender filled the air.

My attendant folded back the sheet, placed her oiled hands on my back, and started working on unknotting the great big stress knots. "Breathe," she said.

"I'm trying," I growled into the face rest. To my surprise, when I concentrated on it, my breathing evened out—and the stress knots couldn't withstand her strong hands. My belly went softer as the tension drained.

My husband sighed his exhale with an almost musical hum.

I wished he could understand. I wasn't trying to keep secrets. But maybe I didn't want to be questioned about every little thing. Maybe I wanted to trust my own judgment rather than feel like I had to run everything by someone else for approval.

I handled the Saltwater Folk all by myself while surfing. And when the ocean dome was about to collapse, I handled that, too.

Was he just hurt that I hadn't shared what happened? Or was he afraid I would slip up?

After a while, his attendant spoke. "Go ahead and turn face-up, please."

The sheets rustled.

He faced the ceiling, looking vulnerable with his shoulders exposed and no glasses on. He turned his head and caught me looking. A tentative smile lifted the corners of his lips.

I gave him the same in return. Then we both had to look straight up while the attendants went to work on our shoulders.

When the massage was complete, they drew the sheets up and slipped out. The bell-like tones of the background music chimed into the quiet.

He sat up first, gathering the sheet around himself like a toga, and put on his glasses.

I hesitated. I hated to break the spell of dreamy relaxation—and in that pause, he stood and came to me.

He held his sheet in place with one hand, not unlike how I'd held the blanket after I lost my pants, and with his free hand, he smoothed his fingers across the top of my forehead and over my hair.

I closed my eyes. His hand felt warm, and smelled of lavender oil. "Pete, we have to get dressed—"

"Hush." His fingertips slid through my curls and massaged my scalp. "While the nice lady was trying to remove my spine with her bare hands, I did some thinking."

My eyes flew open. That didn't sound great. "What do you mean?"

"Hush." His fingers dug into the top of my neck, somehow feeling even better than the professional's touch. "Water's always been your thing, Pep. Now it's just—*official*. You didn't need my advice on what to do out there in the ocean any more than I need yours about how to fill a cavity. If you want to tell me your work stories, I'll listen. But that's up to you. Just know that I'm always interested."

I snuggled my head into his hand and smiled. "I'm hungry."

"Of course you are, you ravenous little beastie. Let's get dressed and get some food."

"But what about getting ready for the Hipocampo?"

He helped me sit up. "Your problem is you make yourself responsible for everything. Rose and Oliver already said they would take care of it. Besides, we have to wait till dark to do anything." He leaned down to my ear. "Wouldn't you like to skip out on responsibility for a few hours, Mrs. Monaco?"

I giggled. "Yes, Mr. Monaco." I slipped into my bathrobe and folded the blanket over my arm. "Do you think they've killed each other yet?"

"Let's find out." He tied his own robe, grabbed his clothes, and opened the door.

Lenore's voice hit me as soon as I stepped into the hallway. "You can't *not* tip!"

"They get paid for working here; why should I pay them, too?"

"Because they're not getting paid enough, you cheapskate!"

Mrs. Millefleur huffed and dug in her bag. "What is this country coming to?" She pulled out two ten-dollar bills and shook them in Lenore's direction. "Happy?"

"Very." She snatched the cash and took off, presumably to find the massage therapists. Or someplace private to stuff the money in her own pocket. It was hard to predict.

"I see the peacemaking process is going well." I said to Mrs. Millefleur.

"Don't start with me, Pepper Monaco. I am rapidly reaching my limit."

"All right, all right, don't bite my head off. Pete and I are going to handle the Hipocampo's dental work tonight. You coming?"

"For heaven's sake, no." She waved a hand. "You young people can take care of it. Get the merman to help, and use Rose's truck, but leave me out of it." She raised an eyebrow as Lenore approached. "I'll already have my hands full."

"Are you talking about me?" said Lenore.

"Only about how I've missed your sweet disposition these long years we've been apart," said Mrs. Millefleur, with sugar-coated acid.

Lenore threw up her hands. "You see what I have to deal with?"

"Honey," said Pete. "We're going to be late for our dinner reservation."

"What dinner reservation? We don't have a—" I stopped when his elbow landed lightly in my side. "A minute to spare. You're right."

He laid his arm over my shoulder and began sidling us toward the spa exit. "A pleasure meeting you ladies. We'll have to do this again soon."

"Very soon," I echoed.

We hurried away before they could stop us.

22

The full moon streaked the waves with silver as they rolled to shore in shades of black and white.

Taillights flashed red on the beach ramp as Rose backed up the trailer to the locked metal barrier. The lights went off, and Rose stepped out.

She came down the ramp, ducked the barrier, and crossed the sand. "Oliver's going to keep the engine running. Obviously, we're not supposed to be parked there."

I hugged myself to warm up—springtime still had its cool nights—and scanned the horizon. "Fisher said they'd meet us here."

Minutes passed. The wind snapped at our clothing, and Rose noticed my uncontrollable shivering. "Here," she said, activating her magic.

Glittery silver stars permeated my clothing and left behind a toasty warmth. "Nice," I said. "Like putting on clothes fresh from the dryer."

Rose stared out to sea. "Couldn't you have moved this thing with the Key of Shadows?"

"What, you want me to walk an unreliable sea monster ten miles through the shadow world?"

"I don't know if it's *ten* miles—"

"Look!" I said. The moonlight had caught on something large beyond the breaking waves.

The Hipocampo rose from the water. It surged forward in its funny way: one part skittering crab, one part galloping horse, one part slithering dragon.

Two figures rode on its back. One of them waved.

"That'll be Fisher and the queen," I said.

"That thing is *way* too big for a truck bed," said Rose.

"Glad you were able to borrow a trailer."

She let out a short laugh. "I wish it had been a closed one. A tarp can only cover so much."

Fisher and the queen dismounted. They each took one side of the Hipocampo's facial fins and led it forward.

I jogged forward to meet them. "The truck's right over there. Do you think it'll get in?"

The Hipocampo made a grumpy-sounding snort.

"Good evening, Lady Pepper," said Fisher, hanging on to the beast's fin as it tossed its head. "We will most assuredly try."

"We brought a bag of fish for it," said the Saltwater Queen, holding out an ancient beach tote that smelled like a seafood counter.

The Hipocampo made a snap at the bag, but the Queen pulled it away just in time.

Rose and I led them to the ramp.

The Saltwater Queen ducked the barrier and climbed into the trailer. Her seaweed skirt and mantle fluttered in the wind. She held out the tote and made coaxing sounds in the merpeople's language of squeaks and clicks.

Fisher, meanwhile, attempted to nudge the Hipocampo to follow her under the barrier by giving it a firm push in the right direction.

The Hipocampo wasn't having it. It backpedaled, easily throwing Fisher off, and made an indignant blowing noise.

"That went well," said Rose.

The queen flung down the fish tote. "Why don't you try, then?"

"Thanks, I will."

Fisher stepped respectfully aside to make way.

The Hipocampo side-eyed Rose as she approached.

"There, now," she said. "Who's a good girl?"

"I thought you called it a boy last time," I said.

"Who cares?" said Rose. "The only thing it understands is tone."

"The sex of the Hipocampo is indeed a mystery," said Fisher.

"See, I was right." Rose patted the Hipocampo's flank. "Who wants to have their boo-boo tooth fixed?"

"Does Oliver like it when you sweet-talk him like that?" I asked.

"Shut up and get the fish."

I jumped into the truck bed and grabbed the tote.

"Get ready to hold out a fish."

"Hang on. Pete gave me some sedation pills. They take a while to kick in, so we better do that first." I pulled out the bottle of pre-counted pills, dumped the pills in my palm, and stuffed them inside the first fish I grabbed.

Rose caught the Hipocampo's rolling gaze, and her eyes flashed silver. "Do you want a fishy?"

The Hipocampo's eyes flashed in return. It nickered.

"Hold it out now, Pepper, and back up."

I held out the pill-stuffed fish. The queen backed up with me until we bumped against the front rail of the trailer.

The Hipocampo sniffed. It confronted the barrier with a look of vexed confusion.

Rose ducked under the barrier. "Come get the fishy, Hipocampo."

It could have fit under the barrier, if it tried. It lifted one of its crab legs and gave the metal barrier an experimental tap.

You could almost see the lights go on in its eyes.

It reared to its full height and crashed both crab legs onto the barrier. The chain snapped with a twang and ricocheted off the barrier itself with a resounding clang. The Hipocampo pranced through the swinging gate with what appeared to be a smug look on its face. Then it launched itself into the trailer bed.

The truck rocked backward. I had to grab the railing so I didn't fall.

Rose quickly jumped into the trailer. "Good Hipocampo. Hipocampo, sit."

It lowered its hindquarters to the trailer floor and wound up its dragonish tail.

"Give it the fish, Pepper."

I threw the slimy thing into its horse mouth.

It chewed happily.

I couldn't help grimacing. No one should have to watch a horse eat a fish.

Fisher joined us in the truck bed.

"We'll stay back here." Rose unfolded a tarp and loosened a coil of rope. "You ride up front with Oliver and give him directions to Pete's office."

I wiped my hands on my shorts, hopped down, closed the trailer gate, and got in the cab. "Hey, Oliver."

"Pepper," he said. "Lovely spring weather we're having." When Rose gave him a thumbs-up from the trailer, he engaged the stick shift and eased the truck into motion.

Most of the businesses along the beach had already closed for the night. Some of them, like Rolling Wave Coffee and the beachside outpost of Sparkle Beach Creamery, still had their neon signs lit.

We were almost to the bridge to the mainland when several short squawking sounds blasted out behind us.

"Is that the Hipocampo?" I said.

Oliver glanced in the rearview mirror. "Not unless it comes equipped with flashing blue lights."

I turned and reached for the cab's back window. Someone had to warn Rose; she was hidden under the tarp and might not be able to see what was coming.

"Don't do that," said Oliver, calmly. "They might think you have a gun."

"What are we going to do? There's a *Hipocampo* back there, in case you didn't notice."

"Leave it to me."

I threw up my hands. "No wonder Rose always wants to slap you."

He barely smiled, but I saw it.

The truck rolled to a stop on the side of the road.

"We are from the university," he said, adjusting his cuffs. "Got it?"

I nodded just as the police officer walked up to the driver's side.

Oliver rolled down the window. "Good evening, officer."

The policeman raised his eyebrows at Oliver's accent. "Not from around here, are you, sir?" He glanced around the interior of the truck. "License and registration?"

Oliver dutifully handed over the documents.

"What's in the trailer?"

"My colleagues and I are from the local university. We are carrying a rescue specimen."

"Is that so?" The officer glanced toward the back.

The Hipocampo drummed its crab legs, making a huge racket and shaking the truck.

Oliver cleared his throat. "Quite. The animal requires treatment before it can be released to the wild."

The officer's hand came away from his weapon. "Can I see it?"

I winced.

"Certainly, sir," said Oliver. "May I . . . ?" He gestured toward the door.

The officer stepped clear.

Oliver raised his voice slightly as he got out, presumably to alert Rose. "Our department chair and two visiting professors are riding with the creature to keep it calm." He moved to the trailer and lifted the edge of the tarp. "Dr. Conleth, the officer would like to examine the specimen."

Rose's head appeared from underneath the tarp. "He would?"

"Don't you bother my Hipocampo!" cried the queen, who, thankfully, was still out of sight under the tarp.

"Dr. Salt is very protective of the animal's well-being," said Oliver.

"She's not from around here either, is she?" the officer said, with a knowing nod.

"You are most perceptive. Dr. Conleth?"

Rose peeled back the covering just enough to reveal the Hipocampo's head.

It pricked its ears up, and its face fins flared wide.

The officer staggered back and issued several non-regulation curse words. "What the hell is that thing?"

"*Hippodamus Miletus*," said Oliver. "Very rare. Highly endangered."

"What do you feed it?"

The Hipocampo leaned out and began to take an interest in the officer's shiny badge.

Rose ducked out of sight and came back up with a fish, which she waved in front of the creature's face.

It took the fish with its teeth and chewed thoughtfully while keeping an eye on the policeman.

"Son of a gun," he said.

"If that's all, officer, we really should get to our lab."

"Would you like an escort?"

I closed my eyes with a wordless prayer to whatever deity took pity on reckless people and Hipocampos.

"It's very kind of you," said Oliver, "but I wouldn't dream of taking an officer of the law away from his rounds."

Rose stared at the policeman. Her eyes flashed silver. "You wouldn't want to get in trouble."

His eyes flickered silver as her magic landed. "I suppose I don't." He took a reluctant step back. "Well, you all have a nice evening. Thanks for letting me see your . . . hippie-whatever-it-is." The policeman retreated with more than one backward glance as he went.

Oliver returned to the cab and slid into the driver's seat.

"*Hippodamus Miletus*? What the hell is that?"

"It's Hippodamus of Miletus, actually. Fifth century Greek philosopher." He revved the engine. "Obscure Greeks are a natural consequence of a British public school education."

Rose waved from the trailer. "I got the tarp tied down. Let's get out of here, tea-and-crumpets."

23

The windows were dark at Monaco Family Dental. Oliver pulled around back and parked the truck by the delivery door, then headed for the front of the building to keep watch.

I got out and used my key to open the delivery door. "Pete?" I called.

"In here," he replied. "I kept the lights low on purpose."

I entered the treatment area. A yellow spotlight lit up a reclining chair and the equipment around it, but the rest of the office was in shadows. "Is this where you're going to do it?"

He rolled over on his wheeled stool. "I thought we could put its head in the chair and run its tail down the hallway."

"You ready?"

"Bring it in."

I picked up the cardboard treasure box and moved it off the floor to a nearby counter on my way out. Better than risking someone tripping on it in the low light.

Outside, Rose, Fisher, and the Saltwater Queen worked to undo the tarp. Between Rose's hypnosis magic and the bag of fish, they managed to lure the Hipocampo out of the trailer and up to the door—where it balked, and refused to go any further.

"Now what?" said Rose.

Fisher took the seafood bag and stepped into the hallway. "Here, Hipocampo. I have more nice fish for you."

The Hipocampo snorted and pulled its head back from the opening.

"Maybe it doesn't like enclosed spaces." I knew something about that after my cave experience. But having my friends and our familiars helped me get through it—and that gave me an idea. "Clove, baby, where are you?"

The silver-clawed otter came running from around the corner of the building, peeping and squeaking all the way.

I picked her up and hugged her.

She poked her nose into my hair and buried her face in my curls.

The Hipocampo took a couple of crab-legged steps forward. Its tail uncoiled. Its rolling eyes steadied and focused on Clove.

I maneuvered Clove out of my hair. Then I took her little paw and waved it. "Say hello to the Hipocampo."

Clove chirped.

The Hipocampo tossed its head in apparent surprise. It blew out a foul-smelling breath.

Clove wiggled in my arms like she wanted to get down.

"You don't think it could hurt her, do you?" I asked Rose.

"Familiars can phase out. I don't think anything physical can touch them if they don't want it to."

I lowered Clove to the ground and stepped into the hallway with Fisher.

Clove scampered to the Hipocampo's foremost crab leg. She went on her hind legs and put her front paws on the knobbly carapace.

The Hipocampo didn't seem to know what to make of this. It lowered its horse head for a better look at the otter. Then it gave a great big sniff.

Clove dropped to all fours and ran in a rapid circle around where the Hipocampo's leg met the ground.

The Hipocampo blinked. It whinnied with a sound almost like a laugh.

Clove dashed to the door and back to the Hipocampo, then back to the door again. It chirped again and hopped inside the threshold.

The Hipocampo lumbered forward and cautiously poked its head through the opening.

Clove ran up and down the hallway like it was PE class. Then she ran up to the Hipocampo, tagged its foreleg, and retreated a foot or so down the hall.

The Hipocampo shuffled forward.

Clove repeated the motion, each time leading the Hipocampo a little farther.

Fisher and I stepped backward, toward the treatment area, to make room. Rose and the queen were silhouetted at the other end of the hall as they came in behind the Hipocampo's fish tail. The second the tail cleared the opening, one of them shut the door behind it.

Clove hopped into the treatment room and leaped onto the reclining chair footrest.

The Hipocampo cautiously peeked into the room.

Pete's eyes widened.

I couldn't blame him. It was one thing to see the beast out in the open; it was another thing altogether to have it crammed into a tiny space with you. "Don't worry," I said. "It has an emotional support otter."

"Oh," he said. "That's good."

Rose and the Saltwater Queen squeezed in and flanked the patient chair. The queen pulled a bone flute from somewhere in her seaweed skirt and began to play a tune. Rose's eyes flashed silver. "Good Hipocampo," she said. "Lie down and listen to the pretty music."

Clove moved from the footrest to the seat itself and launched into a sort of hopping, skipping dance.

Fascinated, the Hipocampo crouched down and balanced its head on the foot rest. Its eyelids lowered sleepily.

"How long has it been?" asked Pete quietly.

"Fifteen minutes at the beach, fifteen minutes with the police, ten minute drive, ten minutes to get it in here. Fifty minutes?"

He nodded. "It should be getting groggy."

The flute music mellowed into a lullaby.

Clove snuggled up near the Hipocampo's nose.

Music, magic, and a fuzzy friend seemed to do the trick. The Hipocampo's eyelids closed. It let out a fish-scented, lip-flapping snore.

"It's out, Pete," I said. "Work fast."

Pete swung into action with long-practiced skill. First, he tucked pads beside the gum to create space and absorb liquid. He placed a vacuum tube beside the tooth to catch dust and drool. The drill made an awful high-pitched sound—we all winced, expecting the Hipocampo to wake—but other than twitching its fish tail, it slept on. He applied the filling and aimed a bright blue curing light at the tooth. After that, it took only a quick polish to wrap up the job.

There was just *something* about watching him work. Deft hands. Smooth, confident, and competent even under the weirdest circumstances. Those little wrinkles around his eyes as he concentrated.

Pretty sexy.

Pete laid aside his instruments, removed the packing, and rolled back. "Done."

"When does the sedation wear off?" said Rose.

"I don't know. I've never sedated a Hipocampo before."

A loud splashing noise carried from down the hall.

"Where's Fisher?" I was already up and moving before anyone answered.

I found him in the waiting room at the other end of the hallway.

He'd upended the entire five-gallon water cooler bottle over his head and stood, smiling, in the center of a large, darkened circle of carpet, lit by the glow of the saltwater aquarium light.

"Fisher, you ninny. Look what you did to the carpet!"

"But I was quite dry, Lady Pepper."

The Saltwater Queen came up behind me.

"See what he did?" I said, expecting sympathy.

Instead, she breezed past Fisher and stood before the aquarium. "Look at that," she said. "Snacks!" She plunged her arm into the tank, snagged a fish, and swallowed it.

I rushed forward and pulled her away. "What are you *doing*? Those are for decoration, not eating!"

"I also am hungry, Lady Pepper," said Fisher politely.

"Eat the fish out of your fish bag!"

"Ah, but they're not as fresh," said the queen.

I pointed at each of them in turn. "No snacking. Got it?" I righted the empty water bottle and used my magic to pull the water out of the carpet. It funneled obediently into the bottle. I'd have to make sure it was used to water the plants instead of going back on the cooler stand.

I looked up just in time to see the queen's arm darting out of the aquarium once more.

She put her hands behind her back and smiled.

It might have been more effective if there wasn't a fin poking out from between her teeth.

I pointed down the hall. "Out. Both of you."

Fisher meekly shuffled away.

The Saltwater Queen remained. She pulled one hand from behind her back. A cream-colored shell dotted with brown speckles lay in her palm. "Here, water witch. This is for you." Faint blue sparkles winked as she put it in my hand. It was an exact twin to the one Lenore had used to summon her to the undersea cave. "If you ever have need of me, put it in the saltwater. I'll come as soon as I can."

I rubbed my thumb over the glossy surface, sparking more of the blue magic. "It's beautiful."

A horse-like snort carried from down the hall.

"That'll be my Hipocampo," she said. She sashayed past, setting her seaweed skirt swinging.

Back in the treatment room, the Hipocampo was waking up. It lifted its head, slowly untucked its crab legs, and heaved itself to its feet. It tossed its head and managed to send the lamp flying sideways. Its groggy, blinkered gaze landed on the treasure box.

Pete stood. "Hey, that's my—"

The Hipocampo took a large bite out of the gold cardboard lid.

"Treasure box," he finished.

24

Since we were running low on clean clothes after all the seawater, fish, and Hipocampo drool, we decided to stop by the house to pick up a few things before heading back to our resort.

I unlocked the front door. The nighttime darkness made the house seem even emptier than when we had left it on the first day.

Pete headed for our room.

"I'm going to get some of my stuff out of the garage," I called. Inside, I opened the door of the bright red dryer and piled the clothes on top in search of wearable items. My own shirt was a bit funky, so I pulled it off and dropped it in the hamper.

Something cold lightly struck my breastbone.

The Key.

The cover had fallen off. Lenore's words popped to mind: *Don't let it touch your skin. And if you do, don't even think about entering another world.* "Don't think of pink manatees," I joked to myself—and pink manatees immediately marched through my mind to the tune of "Heffalumps and Woozles." The idea of another world was impossible to resist. I couldn't help trying to picture it.

And then, just like that, everything changed.

The colorful pile of laundry turned black and white. The red dryer became dark gray. It was like I'd stumbled into an old black-and-white movie. The sound of the air conditioner was gone—but there was a chill in the air that hadn't been there before.

"Uh-oh." Goosebumps rose on my arms, so I lifted one of the weirdly colorless t-shirts and pulled it on. If I got here by thinking of another world, then I should only have to think of the real one to get back. I concentrated on the clean laundry and pictured its true colors. After all, there's nothing realer than laundry.

The shirt I'd just put on disappeared, and I found myself standing in the garage exactly where I had been all along. Everything looked normal again. I hadn't moved, but I'd definitely gone *somewhere.* And the shirt from the shadows didn't come back with me.

I grabbed a new shirt and put it on—carefully hanging the Key on the outside so it wouldn't touch my skin—then I quickly collected what else I needed and headed back into the house.

I found Pete in the bedroom. "Pete, watch this!" I threw down my armful of clothes on the bed, grabbed the Key, and thought of the black-and-white world.

Poof! I was there again, only Pete wasn't. I spun around. "Pete? Pete?"

No husband. I must have left him behind in the real world.

Oh, right—that's why Mrs. Millefleur was holding on to Lenore before I took the Key away. If you were touching someone, you took them with you. I marveled at the strange black-and-white look of the bedroom before returning to find Pete clutching a clean pair of underwear to his chest.

"You scared me!"

"Sorry, sorry! I was so excited I didn't even think. Wanna try?" I held out my hand.

He slowly lowered the pair of underwear. "Are you sure that thing's *safe*?"

"No."

He threw the underwear at me.

I dodged. "If Lenore can use it safely, I'm sure we can too."

"I don't know . . ."

"We could sneak over to the neighbors and steal that yard sign you hate."

His eyes lit up. "'No Trespassing: We're Tired of Hiding the Bodies'? You mean it?"

I nodded.

"Mmm." His eyes closed. "Talk petty vengeance to me."

I put my arms around his neck. "I bet they'll be *so mad* . . ."

He swayed like we were slow dancing—then opened his eyes and planted a kiss on my head. "Sold. Let's do it before I change my mind."

"Come on." I headed to the front door.

Pete followed. "Are you sure we should—"

"Don't think. Just hold my hand and I'll take you there. Like the Madonna song!" I hummed a bar of "Like a Prayer" and took Pete's hand in mine. I pictured the house, the neighborhood, everything in Sparkle Beach in black and white.

This time, Pete came with me into the shadows.

I opened the front door.

"Whoa," he said.

A whitish light like an overcast sky lit up the street where only streetlights shone before. Although everything was as neat and orderly as our real street, the black-and-white stillness made it look like an episode of *The Twilight Zone*. Everything was so quiet I couldn't help but lower my voice. "This is kinda creepy."

"You're telling me." He gripped my hand more firmly.

We stepped outside. Neither one of us closed the door. Somehow, it seemed better to have an open door at our backs. We walked down the driveway, same as we had a thousand times before, only not in an alternate reality. Then we turned toward our next-door neighbors' house.

You had to give them credit for finding so many ways to be annoying. It took a while to realize they'd been pirating our wi-fi. By the time we'd figured that out, they'd also made a habit of letting their dog poop on our lawn. Even confronting them about the poop didn't stop them from trying to recruit us for their harebrained multilevel marketing schemes. They didn't have a drop of shame in their entire bodies—so the ugly sign, when they added it to their lawn decor, wasn't exactly a surprise.

"You're sure nobody's home?" said Pete.

"Nobody's anywhere. It's just us."

We crossed their lawn and faced the sign, which hung on a tree trunk.

Pete glanced over his shoulder as if someone might come up at any moment. "Let's just grab it and go."

"Hang on," I said. "I don't think it works that way. I put on a shirt from the shadow world just a few minutes ago and it disappeared the second I came back."

"So none of this is real?"

I shrugged. "Not real enough to come back with us."

"How do we take it, then?"

"We have to pop out and grab it."

"Pop out and grab it? Are you kidding? What will the neighbors think when they see us winking in and out of existence?"

"Since when do you care what the neighbors think about anything? Besides, have you *seen* their recycling bins? They drink so much no one would believe a word they say."

"You didn't tell me that before."

"About their recycling bins?"

"No, about how we would actually have to make an appearance to pull this off."

"It didn't occur to me, okay? It will only take a sec. It'll be fine."

"Pepper . . ."

"You want to wait here while I do it?"

"What? No!" He shuddered. "I'm coming with you."

I patted his hand in mine. "It'll be dark. Don't worry." I held the Key and wished to go back to the real world.

We appeared on their lawn in exactly the same spot, only now the white light was gone, replaced by yellow streetlight. The neighbor's blinds were open, and a TV flickered inside.

I seized the sign and pulled. "It's stuck!" It wasn't hanging on a nail—it was screwed into the tree.

"Let me." Pete hauled on the sign, twisting it this way and that.

"It's no good," I said. "We better go back."

"Just one more—"

I added my strength to his. The metal at the top of the sign gave way with a snap. We both tumbled backward; the sign bounced off the tree and landed in the grass.

The blinds twitched.

"Time to go." I scrambled for the sign, grabbed Pete's hand, and pictured the neighbor-less shadow world.

The streetlights went off and the TV light disappeared. The green grass turned gray and the sky turned white.

And we had the sign.

We both laughed as we ran back to our house. Inside, I grabbed Pete and took us from the shadow world to the real one, trading silence and shadows for colors and life.

"We did it!" He held his hand up for a high five.

I slapped his hand and did an impromptu dance right there in the entryway.

He took the sign and paraded it down the hallway. When he got to the living room, he carefully set the sign on top of a shelf like a hunting trophy. "How soon do we have to be back at the hotel, Mrs. Monaco?"

"What do you mean, 'how soon'? We can get there whenever we want." I flopped on the couch and stretched out luxuriously.

He turned and met my gaze with a flirtatious smile and a gleam in his eye. "Good."

25

The next day, Queenie called a meeting of the Sparkle Beach witches at Suntan Queen. We were lucky to have a witch in our crew with a space large enough to fit all of us. The conference room held Queenie's treasured surfboard collection, everything from an old solid wood board to newer innovations like the short board, the hollow board, and several curved board variations. I caressed a single-fin solid balsa wood board—a Bob Simmons original. "You sure we can't take this one out for a spin?"

"That would be like hanging a Renoir on your porch, darling. It's simply too old to withstand it." Queenie positioned a clear pitcher next to some bagels and spreads, and an assortment of fruit, cheese, and meat on a tray.

Luella and Raphael entered, followed by Rose and Oliver.

Queenie looked up. "Where are Hilda and Lenore?"

"They're coming," said Rose. "They were still arguing over the radio station presets, so we left them to it."

We helped ourselves to breakfast. I'd already eaten, but after the excitement of last night, the everything bagels were calling my name. By the time I'd polished off mine with extra cream cheese, Mama arrived.

She looked around the room. "Where's the trouble twins?"

"Arguing in the car," said Oliver.

Mama made a disbelieving noise and sat next to Queenie. "Hilda probably wants to make an entrance."

Mrs. Millefleur swept into the room, followed by Lenore.

"See?" said Mama.

Mrs. Millefleur took the empty seat on the other side of Queenie. "See what?"

"Nothing." Mama grinned.

"I haven't time for your nonsense," said Mrs. Millefleur. "Lenore, the notes."

Lenore, who had remained standing, rounded on her sister. "Don't boss me."

Mrs. Millefleur took a slow breath. "Lenore, *please*. The notes."

Lenore reached into her bag and removed an entire pile of sticky notes covered in writing. She leaned over the conference table and began laying them out, one at a time, in neat rows like a spreadsheet.

"What's that?" said Luella.

Mama held up a finger for silence. Her sharp gaze darted over the grid of paper squares. "Queenie—"

"I know, Belinda," Queenie said, her voice tight.

"Wait," I said, "You only showed me one of those. The one with—"

"Hilda's address. Yes," said Lenore. "These are the rest of them."

The rest of them? That didn't sound good.

Oliver frowned and caught Mrs. Millefleur's gaze. She gave a single nod.

Well, they all seemed to be catching on to something. I leaned forward to read some of the names on the sticky notes.

Hildegarde Millefleur.

Belinda Campbell.

Queenie Russell.

Tuesday Lamour.

And a whole bunch of other names I didn't know. "What is this, a witch Rolodex? Where's the rest of us?"

"These are known witches. You are new," said Oliver.

"You don't *want* to be known," said Mrs. Millefleur.

"Not by this guy," added Lenore, in the first instance possibly ever of her agreeing with her sister on anything.

"Why not?" I said. I was slightly miffed that I wasn't famous enough to get my own sticky note.

Lenore sank into an open chair. "Because he's Robert Wickham. The former head of Elozent Industries, in Miami."

"The head of whose-a-vent?"

"They went under, didn't they? Like, a year ago?" said Raphael.

"Oh, *that* Elozent." I'd seen it on the news, but it didn't make sense why the big boss of some failed company would have a list of witches. "I don't get it." I looked to Luella and Rose, but they shrugged.

"When I lived in Miami, I worked for Elozent," said Lenore. "I didn't know it at the time—none of us 'regular' people did—but the executives had been hollowing out the company from the inside for years. The record profits were a sham. When it was all about to collapse, the executives raided the employee investment and pension funds to stock their own piggy banks. The rest of us were left to twist in the wind. I was *this close* to retiring."

"Literally one week away," added Mrs. Millefleur.

Mama shook her head. "Bet they didn't go to jail. That type never does."

"Not for lack of trying on my part," said Lenore. "Thanks to the arrival of the Key of Shadows"—she shot her sister a look, which Mrs. Millefleur studiously ignored—"I was able to break into the CEO's house to search for evidence."

"And steal things," said Mrs. Millefleur.

"Who's telling this story, you or me?" When Mrs. Millefleur didn't say anything else, Lenore continued. "I didn't find anything incriminating in his house, so I decided to break into the Elozent high-rise. At that point, even the Key of Shadows couldn't get me to the high floor where I needed to go—electricity doesn't work in the Shadows, and neither do elevators." She shook her head. "No way I was going to climb thirty-one flights of stairs."

"How did you get up there?" said Luella.

"I flew." She waited a beat while that information sank in. "Years ago, I overheard Hilda talking about where the witches hung out in Miami. So I went there and tried to recruit an air witch to help me fly up. Nothing doing. Instead, she told me about the Eye of the Elements, and how it was currently on display in a downtown museum. The icing on the cake, of course, was the fact that it was from Robert

Wickham's personal collection. The Key of Shadows made stealing it a cinch."

"Nice," I said. Then I realized I'd gotten a little too caught up in the story. I was supposed to be mad at Lenore, not cheering her on.

"With the Eye of the Elements, I flew up to the right floor. With the Key of Shadows, I broke into his office. I expected to find his second set of books in the safe, to prove what happened to the money. Instead, I found a book of names and addresses. I couldn't take it out of the shadows, because you can't take things out of the shadows that come from the shadows—but I wrote down as many as I could on a pack of sticky notes I had in my pocket."

Rose made a soft sound of understanding. "You saw your sister's name."

"And the names of her old friends," said Lenore, glancing at Mama and Queenie.

"Did you come back to check on her, or steal her powers?" I said.

"Both," said Mrs. Millefleur.

Lenore swept all of us with a defiant look. "If I had had my sister's hypnosis powers, I would have been able to grab Robert Wickham by the throat and *make* him tell me where he hid the money and the accounting books—*and* why he was keeping a list of witches in his safe."

Mrs. Millefleur rolled her eyes. "That's not how it works, Lenore. You can't just *make* people do things."

"Hilda tried it often enough, she would know," said Mama.

"Your editorializing is entirely unnecessary, Belinda," said Mrs. Millefleur.

"She is right, though," said Rose. "You can't use magic to make someone do something they're dead set against. It has to be at least somewhat aligned with what they want."

Mama propped her hands behind her head and directed her piercing gaze at Lenore. "You could have gone to him and ratted your sister out. Maybe then he would have given you your money back."

"You think I would have handed my sister over like that?"

Expressions around the table showed that yes, we all thought that.

"Robert Wickham can burn in hell," said Lenore. "If anybody's going to give my sister a hard time"—she paused and aimed a half-threatening, half-affectionate smile at her sister—"it's going to be me."

"That's . . . weirdly touching," said Rose. "In a sick, twisted kind of way."

"You could have put him in the shadows until he talked," I said.

"I didn't want to give the game away. Not to him. If I had been able to hypnotize him, he never would have known about it."

Oliver coolly traced an elegant finger under the nearest row of sticky notes. "This information is from over a year ago," he said. "By now, he could have the identities of even more witches."

"What could he do?" said Luella.

Queenie twisted a ring on her finger. "Oh, darlings—in the wrong hands, this could change *everything*. Imagine what an intelligence agency might do with this information. Or the military. Even tabloid coverage could ruin lives."

"This is why we have never been centralized," added Mrs. Millefleur. "Witches work alone, or at most, within a small community. The less we are connected, the less we are vulnerable."

The radioactively-colored sticky notes drew all eyes.

Some of us weren't on the list—but what if we were, somewhere, and we just didn't know it yet?

What if I was on it?

What if he knew where I *lived*?

I crossed my arms. "So far no one's telling me how we're going to stop this guy from turning all of us into targets."

"Though he would like it to be our disadvantage," said Queenie, "our connection to each other is also our greatest strength."

Mrs. Millefleur nodded. "Robert Wickham, on the other hand, has several weaknesses with which to contend. One: Any attempt to reveal a conspiracy of witches must be handled with great delicacy. Anything less than airtight evidence will get him laughed out of wherever he presents it, if not involuntarily committed for his trouble. Two: The 'creative accounting' at Elozent Industries most likely carries significant jail time. Three: Things of value, such as evidence and money, are—as Lenore could tell you—only as secure as where you keep them. And when you have a group of witches involved, well . . . that's not necessarily very secure at all." A tight smile compressed her lips. "Somewhere within those weaknesses lies our solution."

"Coming up with diabolical plans is what Hilda does for fun," said Mama. "That's why you don't want to get on her bad side."

"You have come up with your share of diabolical plans, Belinda."

"'Course I have. You don't want to get on my bad side, neither. Or Queenie's, even if she likes to act like she wouldn't hurt a fly."

Queenie smiled and inclined her head, acknowledging the compliment.

"But couldn't he just hand over whatever he has to someone else and let them cause trouble?" asked Luella.

"Unlikely," said Oliver. "As Mrs. Millefleur stated, it's quite a delicate matter. And he is probably not inclined to trust anyone enough to share the information, or the glory of revealing it."

Mrs. Millefleur raised one finger. "There is one problem, though." When everyone was looking at her, she continued. "Robert Wickham is—at this very moment—on his way to Sparkle Beach. For the regatta."

My chest constricted. "Oh, my God." I stood, knocking my chair backwards. "I have to go. I have to go make sure—" I stumbled toward the door, unsure of what I would do, only that it would start with finding Robert Wickham and throwing him in deep water and never letting him up.

Rose and Luella sprang up and intercepted me.

"Pepper," said Luella. "I know. I have a kid, too, remember?"

I whirled to face Mrs. Millefleur. "You saved this until now? You couldn't have led with that little tidbit of information?"

"We must keep cool heads—"

"Screw that. I'm going to go check on my kids."

26

I pushed the doors open and took the stairs two at a time to get to the ground floor. Back in my SUV, I called my dad. "Come on, pick up." I struck the steering wheel when the call went to voicemail.

Of course they had to be fine. The witch-hunting CEO couldn't possibly be in town yet.

Someone knocked on my window.

I jumped so hard I dropped the phone and nearly hit my head on the roof.

Luella gave a tentative wave. Behind her, Rose waved, too.

I rolled down the window. "You scared me half to death!"

"We came to check on you," said Luella.

"You didn't look okay," added Rose.

I banged my forehead into the steering wheel. "I just found out I'm on a list and some psycho rich guy wants to turn me over to Cigarette Smoking Man on *The X-Files*."

My phone rang. I scrambled for it, dropped it, let out a few curse words, and picked it up. "Dad? Hello?"

"Hi, honey. You okay? You sound terrible."

Obviously I *was* terrible—at hiding my feelings. "I'm fine. Are *you* okay?"

"Everything's great. How's your vacation going? Getting homesick yet?"

I let out a weak laugh. "You got me, Dad."

"Me and the boys were gonna go fishing at the pond around the corner. Did you need something?"

"Can I talk to Rocky and Kevin for a second?"

After a fumbling noise, Kevin got the phone. "Mom! You'll never guess! Grandpa let us binge watch all the *Seinfeld* episodes we wanted and we ate pizza for breakfast and now we're going fishing so I gotta go, love you, bye!"

"I love you! Can I talk to—" A click sounded over the connection. "Rocky," I finished. Kevin had already hung up. I lowered the phone and stared at it.

"Can we get in?" said Luella.

For a moment, I'd forgotten they were even there. I hit the unlock button.

Rose jumped in the back, and Luella took the shotgun seat.

"This is so much worse than I thought it would be," I said.

"What is?" said Luella.

"This. Everything. Being a witch. Going on vacation without the kids. I thought it would be all fun and excitement, and now—" My throat hurt. I had to swallow before I could continue. "Now I just want to go home. I miss them. I miss their messy rooms, and their arguments, and their stupid video games—"

"Oh, Pepper." Luella patted my shoulder.

"And now I've put them in danger . . ."

Despite being in a closed-up car, a wind came from nowhere.

Two pointed white ears appeared in my rearview mirror. Zephyr squeezed between the seats and joined Luella.

A plaintive meow sounded from behind my seat. Horatio leapt onto the center console, stepped down onto my thigh, and then settled like a fuzzy hot water bottle on my lap.

Something moved around my ankles.

"Clove?" I peered below the steering wheel.

She poked her head up by my knee. Her bright, inquisitive eyes shone. She hoisted herself up, climbed over Horatio, and went on her hind legs to place her silver-clawed front paws on my shoulder so she could nuzzle my cheek with her nose.

I patted Clove with one hand, and Zephyr with the other. Horatio gazed up at me with golden eyes.

Furry friends everywhere.

Not to mention my un-furry friends, who had followed me out to the car to make sure I was all right.

"Have you eaten?" said Luella.

"No," I said, trying and failing to cover a sniffle. "Not since that bagel, anyway."

"Oh, no, she's starving!" said Rose.

I laughed before burying my face in my hands.

"Listen," said Luella. "We're going to take this guy *out*."

"Like yesterday's garbage," said Rose.

I looked up. "You're sure?"

Luella nodded decisively. "Drive, woman. To Shelly's Place!"

Zephyr, Horatio, and Clove jumped into the back seat with Rose.

I drove. There was no arguing with Luella when she decided to take charge. Shelly's Place was only a few minutes away across the bridge. The mermaid sign startled me—I'd seen it a thousand times, but I'd never once dreamed that mermaids could actually be real, or that I'd get to *be* one, even if it was just temporary.

"You're smiling," said Rose. "Are you thinking about a triple play platter?"

"I knew this was a good idea," said Luella.

We got out, and the familiars wandered off together, presumably for their own mischief.

Shelly's Place was the same as always. Twinkling Christmas lights and fishnets hanging from the wall. A striped surfboard hanging overhead. Classic rock on the radio.

I breathed a tiny bit easier.

We grabbed a table and agreed to go alcohol-free for clear thinking.

"So," said Rose. "What can we do to get this guy?"

Luella sipped her Coke before responding. "If we could prove Robert Wickham took all that money out of his company before it went down, we could get him locked up."

"We need his accounting books," I said.

"Wouldn't law enforcement have already seized them?" Luella asked.

I shook my head. "They seized the company's official set of books. We need the other ones. The ones Lenore was trying to find. When you do 'creative accounting,' you have to keep a second set of books for yourself so you can keep track of what's really going on. The downside is . . . you've kept track of what's really going on. So if anyone gets their hands on those, you've written your own ticket to jail. That's why Lenore wanted them in the first place."

"Do you think he keeps that set of books with him?" said Rose.

"Maybe. If not, we could try beating it out of him."

"Pepper!" said Luella.

"Although someone else would have to do it—I can't stand the sight of blood." I smiled to show I was at least partially kidding. Personally, I would have preferred to drown him. Less messy that way.

"So we get the incriminating books off him, if we can. What if that doesn't work?" said Rose. "He still has that list of witches."

"Mrs. Millefleur said he had to be really careful how he presented the information, or people would think he was crazy."

There was a plastic fish on the wall I'd never noticed before, mounted on a branch of driftwood. I'd read a fish story just the other night, in that book of Russian folktales Rocky left on his bedside table. "Fish in the trees," I muttered to myself, trying to bring it to mind. "Fish in the forest!" I cried.

Rose and Luella looked at me like I'd lost my mind.

"'Fish in the Forest.' It's an old Russian folktale. Rocky has this whole collection of folktales we bought for him when he was littler. Before we left for our trip, he had them all piled up on his bedside table. We read one of them the night before our vacation."

Luella made a confused face.

"And this has . . . *what* to do with our present situation?" said Rose.

"I'm getting to it," I said. "In the story, a man finds a pot of gold in a field. He takes it home and shows it to his wife. They hide the gold under the floorboards. But then the man has second thoughts—his wife is a terrible gossip, can't keep a secret, and if she knows about the gold, she'll tell everyone. Someone will steal it or the king will seize it for his own.

"So the man makes a plan. He tells his wife that the next day, they're going to get fish in the forest. She says he's silly—that you don't get fish in the forest—and he just tells her to wait and see."

"The next morning he gets up early, alone. He takes a basket of fish and a basket of cakes into the forest. He puts the fish and cakes on the trees. He kills a rabbit and puts it on a fishing line in the stream. Then, he takes his wife into the forest and pretends all of it is totally normal. She picks the cakes and fish off the trees and puts them in a basket. He hauls in the fishing line and shows her how he caught a rabbit in the river. 'Oh yes,' he says, 'the river is the best place to catch rabbits. The forest is the best place to pick fish and cakes.'"

"The day after that, the king calls them in. He's heard about the gold. The man protests and says there is no gold, that his wife is known for saying foolish things. And who pipes up but the angry wife, saying, 'Of course he has the gold! He found it the day before we fished for rabbits in the river and picked fish and cakes in the forest!'"

"And no one believes her." Rose stirred her drink with the straw. "So . . . you want to hang fish in trees?"

"No, I want to make this Robert Wickham guy seem unreliable so no one will believe him if he starts talking about witches."

The triple play platter arrived, and we all helped ourselves to mozzarella cheese sticks, potato skins, and fried chicken tenders.

Luella swirled a chicken tender in the honey mustard sauce. "It would have to be something in public."

"Something with witnesses," I said.

Rose's brow wrinkled. "'Exit, pursued by a bear.'"

Luella and I looked at her.

"It's from Oliver's favorite play, *The Winter's Tale.*"

"And?"

"A character gets chased offstage and mauled to death by a bear."

"Nice." I dunked a mozzarella stick in marinara sauce. "Can we borrow Oliver's bear for some mauling?"

"If we wanted him dead, there are less messy ways," said Rose. "Ask Lenore."

"What if we weren't trying to maul him? What if we just wanted to *scare* him?" Fish and cakes and bears danced through my head like holiday sugarplums. There was an answer somewhere in there. "What if . . . what if he *thought* he was being chased by a bear, but no one else could see the bear?"

"You mean, the bear is the fish?" said Rose.

"Exactly. What if he saw something that wasn't there, and freaked out?"

"He can't see a familiar, though," Luella said. "Not unless he's cooperating, like Pete or Rose's sister did. And that would defeat the purpose."

"What if we could *make* him see it?"

"That would take an awful lot of power," said Rose. "Even Mrs. Millefleur, as far as we know, hasn't managed to do that."

"What if we boosted your power with the fire opal? What if . . . what if the Eye of the Elements could be used, too? What if we threw everything we had behind it?"

"We don't have the Eye of the Elements," Rose pointed out. "The Sweetwater Queen does."

"Not for long." I grabbed my purse and rummaged in it for money to pay. "Otherwise I have to explain to my husband why we have to join the witch-ness protection program."

27

No one wants to end a vacation with the kind of conversation I was about to have. The elevator up felt like I was being slingshotted into the sun, most likely to burn into a crisp. I stepped out at our floor and had to stop myself from diving back into the elevator.

I slid the electronic key into the lock. A muted buzz and click sounded before I was able to turn the handle and enter. "Pete? I'm back."

Only then did I register the sound of the shower.

I had a little reprieve.

I put my purse down next to Pete's wallet and keys. His stuff sat on top of a shiny brochure folded in two with only the hotel logo visible. I glanced toward the bathroom, then slid the brochure out from under the wallet, muffling the keys with my other hand as I did so. I lifted the brochure and unfolded it, revealing text in a swirling ornamental font.

"Vivacqua Resort . . . vow renewal?" My hand flew to my mouth. "Oh, my God."

The shower clicked off.

I hastily refolded the brochure and shoved it under the wallet and keys, then dove onto the bed in an attempt to look casual.

Pete emerged, rubbing his hair with a towel. "You're back! How'd your meeting go?"

I sat up. Some things were too hard to discuss lying down. "Fine, but—there are some problems."

He pulled up a chair from the table by the windows. "Problems?"

I told him about the sticky notes and Robert Wickham. How if I wasn't on the witch list now, I soon would be—and I didn't know what any of it would mean for us as a family.

"And that's all I know," I finished. My gaze slid helplessly over to the vow renewal brochure. He'd probably want a divorce now, after all the trouble I'd caused. I couldn't even *Bell, Book and Candle* my way out by giving up my powers.

Or could I? Mrs. Millefleur had given hers to Rose, even though it ended up being temporary.

My husband was silent and motionless in the chair. He gazed out the window into the far distance.

"Pete—maybe I should give up my powers."

He blinked and turned his gaze toward me. "What?"

"Mrs. Millefleur did it before, with Rose, and then Rose did it too, and I haven't done it, but I bet Queenie and I could figure it out—"

"Pepper."

"And it would be worth it, wouldn't it, for peace of mind so we would never have to worry about—"

"*Pepper.*"

"Hm?"

"I'm insulted."

"I—what?"

He stood and swiftly crossed the room to where my purse and his wallet and keys lay. He picked up the brochure. "This isn't how I wanted to do this, but—" He carried it to where I was sitting. He went down on one knee and unfolded the glossy paper. "I've been meeting with the event staff here about a vow renewal. Look." His finger, usually so steady, shook slightly as he pointed to the inner pages. "Cake. Flowers. The whole works."

"Why are you telling me this now?" My voice trembled.

"Because, you goose, you really think I'd ask you to give up your magic? *I love you.* You are who you are. If I can't handle the Pepper magic, I don't deserve you." He laid the brochure aside and took my hand. "Knowing what I know now—that you're a witch, that you can summon a magical otter, that someone wants to put you on a list for it—doesn't change a thing. Pepper, will you marry me again?"

It was like getting thrown off the surfboard except on dry land. Shock hit me, even though I'd already seen the brochure on the dresser. I looked away, over Pete's shoulder, where there was a view of the beautiful, breezy spring day, strangely silent thanks to the thick hotel window.

Were we different now than when we first married? Yes.

Did it matter? Yes.

But *how* did it matter?

We *had* changed. We'd grown as people—sharpened in some ways, softened in others—becoming more and more ourselves with every year that passed.

I looked into Pete's eyes and calm spread over me like temperature-controlled air from the vent.

The me I'd become loved the man he'd become. I dropped to the floor beside him and threw my arms around him. "I will!"

He laughed with relief. "For a second I thought you were going to say 'no.'"

I giggled. "You never thought that."

"Come on," he said, releasing me and standing. He held his hand out. "We've only got one day left without the kids. Let's make it count."

"You mean celebrate?" I said, letting him pull me to my feet. "There's this really good-looking apple tart at the restaurant downstairs I haven't tried yet—but we should probably ruin Robert Wickham's life, first."

"We'll earn that dessert," said Pete. "Tell me what you want to do."

I stood on the shoreline below the Vivacqua with Pete by my side. "I haven't tried this before," I said. "I'm not sure if it will work." I waded into the water with the Saltwater Queen's shell. I held it tightly and submerged it beneath the waves. "Saltwater Queen, I need you."

Blue magic traced over the shell like lines of sunlight on the bottom of a swimming pool. An echo of the light burst outward, laser-like, then faded.

I splashed ashore. "That's it, I guess. Now we wait."

We sat together on the sand, facing the horizon, watching the pelicans cruise over the breakers. Five minutes passed, then ten.

"Maybe she's not coming," I said.

"She could be anywhere," said Pete. "It's only been a few minutes."

I dug in the sand, creating messy little castles to keep my hands busy.

"Look!" said Pete.

A head broke the surface a few dozen yards out. A hand waved. Both disappeared as the figure dove under the waves.

"It's her. It has to be." I scrambled up.

When the head popped up again, I could clearly see the Saltwater Queen's short locks studded with shells. I waved and ran forward, dancing through the water as it slid over the sand.

She rose from the waves. Her seaweed mantle and skirt dripped seawater. "You called, water witch?"

"Hello, Salty."

Her color-shifting blue gaze held mine. "What do you need me for, then?"

"Your Sweetie wants to give you a present." This was a fabrication—but I would take care of that shortly.

"A present? My *Sweetie*?"

"You know—the Sweetwater Queen. Sweetie."

She put her hands on her hips and laughed. "Water witch, I would do anything you ask, just to see you call her that to her face."

I grinned. "I've been saving that one up for a while."

"She wants to give me a gift?"

"Yes."

"I've got nothing for her, though."

"Can you get something nice by tonight?"

"That I can, if you want me to."

"Good. Make sure it's something special. Meet us at the southside cove at moonrise."

Since I had no way of getting back to the Sweetwater Queen in her underground court, I had to rely on Fisher to carry the message.

He'd taken to hanging out at Queenie's probably more than was healthy.

Pete and I crossed the pool deck and found him spinning lazily inside a unicorn pool floatie. He had a hurricane glass of frosty orange slush topped with a pineapple slice. "Lady Pepper! And her boon companion!" He lifted the glass. "Would you join me in the pool?"

"Just what we need—a drunk merman," I said to Pete. "Fisher, get out of the pool."

"I shall endeavor to do so, lady witch." He spun around a few more times, then pushed off in the direction of the stairs. He climbed out with perfect balance—and the floatie still around his waist.

When Fisher joined us on the deck, Pete took his glass and sniffed at the contents. "He's not drunk. There's not a whiff of alcohol."

Fisher smiled. "That? The Lady Queenie assured me it was entirely free of spirits. A virgin, she called it. She said it was perfect for me."

Pete shrugged, tipped the glass back, and smacked his lips.

"Uh-huh," I said. "Anyway . . . I need you to get your mom out of her cave and up to the bay tonight. At moonrise."

"What for, Lady Pepper?"

"To make peace with your other mom. And—this is important—tell her the reason for the occasion is because the Saltwater Queen wants to give her a present."

His face brightened. "A present! She will be most pleased."

"And, Fisher? She should have something nice—something *really* nice—to give the Saltwater Queen in return. Can you manage that?"

He threw his arms around me, enfolding me in a damp hug. "For you, Lady Pepper, I would brave any terror—even convincing my Mother."

28

The Saltwater Queen and her motley crew of scruffy, blue-tattooed Folk emerged from the waves onto the thin beach that lined the southern edge of the bay. Two of them carried something large wrapped in the tarp we'd used on the night of the Hipocampo's dental appointment.

The two Saltwater Folk carefully laid the package on the sand and stepped back.

The Saltwater Queen scanned the bay. "Is she coming, water witch?"

"She'll be right here. Fisher told me she wanted to make it extra special." I prayed that Fisher had done his part—because if he hadn't, we were going to have mermaid World War III right there on the sand.

The wavelets lapped at our feet while we waited.

The Saltwater Queen shifted uncomfortably. "I knew it wouldn't work. We'll go."

"Wait!" I pointed toward the western side of the bay. "There they are."

Green light broke the surface before the Sweetwater Folk did. The Sweetwater Queen emerged in a garment of fresh flowers lit by streams of green-glowing water.

"Showoff," said the Saltwater Queen—but she said it under her breath, so her counterpart couldn't hear, and then hastily fluffed her hair.

One of the Sweetwater Folk carried a covered basket ashore.

The two queens faced each other. Their eyes glowed faintly with their blue and green magic. In the darkness, Fisher's did, too, except his were a sort of teal in-between shade.

The Sweetwater Queen lifted a graceful hand. Her attendant hurried forward and lifted the lid from the basket. A warm, honey-colored glow spilled over the Queen's arms as she reached into the basket with both hands and slowly brought out her gift: a giant whelk shell.

Glittery, spiky yellow crystals burst from the inside of the shell like dragon teeth. Each crystal extended a good six inches from the shell opening. Every facet cast a tiny flame of yellow light. The little lights traveled over us as if they were fireflies.

It was, without a doubt, one of the most marvelous treasures I'd ever seen. Like something out of a museum. One-of-a-kind. The rarest of the rare.

She held the crystal-filled shell out. "For you, Saltwater Queen."

The Saltwater Queen stepped forward.

Their fingers touched as the whelk passed from one queen to the other. The Saltwater Queen cradled the shell in one arm, and with her other hand, she traced the crystals' contours. Her gaze met her counterpart's. "A fine gift, to be sure." With great gravity, she turned and offered the shell to Fisher, who took it with care.

The Saltwater Queen herself removed the tarp from the gift she'd brought, revealing a great white curve of bone. Silver strings flashed in the moonlight.

It kind of resembled Rose's harp—if Rose's harp were made of bone and wire.

The Saltwater Queen kneeled on the sand, propped the harp on her shoulder, and began to play.

The notes pinged into the night air with a melody that spoke of loss and longing. The final measures had the sound of a question, with a light touch of hope. Even when the strings stopped ringing, the sound resonated inside me.

The Sweetwater Queen sank to her knees, mirroring her counterpart's position.

Their eyes met.

Without looking away, the Saltwater Queen moved the harp to the side. One attendant from each side rushed forward, and together, they lifted the harp out of the way.

The space between the queens lay clear.

Both of them closed their eyes and extended their hands, but did not touch. Blue light crackled over the Saltwater Queen, green light over the Sweetwater Queen.

"What are they doing?" I whispered to Fisher. "Are they summoning Hipocampos? Are they going to fight?"

"They have not spoken in many years," he said, "but they do not need to speak. When they are one with the water, they can read each other's hearts." He gripped the shell tighter.

Slowly their magic extended closer to the other, then to the water of the bay.

What must it be like, to be in such close contact that you don't even need words? Would it hurt? Would it be a relief? Would you ever be the same after seeing someone like that? After they see *you* that clearly?

A single emerald tear slid down the cheek of the Sweetwater Queen.

Water washed up around them, swirling in their individual colors. The edge of the wavelets turned a blue-green sheen.

The Saltwater Queen cried out, half in pain, half in joy—and phosphorescence spread across the bay like a blanket of opals.

The assembled merpeople knelt as one.

The queens opened their eyes. They smiled at each other, a little bashfully. Then the Saltwater Queen lunged across the distance separating them, sank her fingers into her Sweetie's tangled locks, and planted a kiss on her like a sailor home from a long voyage.

The Sweetwater Queen's eyebrows rose in surprise. After a few moments, she playfully shoved her counterpart away. "We are not to be seized at will, Saltwater Queen."

The Saltwater Queen grinned. "Ah, Sweetie, I could not help myself."

"We are not 'Sweetie.' We are the Sweetwater Queen."

"You could call her 'Salty,'" I said.

The Sweetwater Queen gave her mermaid love a mischievous look. "We prefer 'Old Salt.'"

"Old Salt! I'll Old Salt you, you saucy princess!"

They collapsed into the shallows, giggling and splashing. The Saltwater and Sweetwater Folk cheered.

Fisher replaced the shell of crystals in the basket and turned to me. "I was not wrong, Lady Pepper. A thousand favors I owe you."

"Can I call in one of them?"

"But ask, and I obey."

"May I please borrow the Eye of the Elements from your mom?"

"Come," he said. "We will ask while she is in a fine mood."

We splashed forward.

The queens had transformed into full mermaids. They lay in the shallows and flipped their tails, idly sending drops of water flying through the air. The Saltwater and Sweetwater Folk waded into the water around their respective queens, changing forms as soon as the water was deep enough.

"My Mothers," said Fisher with a slight bow, "the Lady Pepper would like to ask a favor."

"Say on, water witch," replied the Saltwater Queen.

"My family is in danger."

The queens traded a concerned look.

"There's a bad man coming to town who's hunting for magic users. If I'm not on his list by now, I will be soon. Me, my family, and all the other witches are at risk of being exposed."

"What would you have us do?" asked the Sweetwater Queen.

"My friends and I are going to need all the help we can get. I'm asking that you return the Eye of the Elements to us, so we can use it to take him down."

The Sweetwater Queen regarded me calmly. "We will return the Eye—"

I smiled in relief.

"On one condition." Her eyes glinted green in the darkness. "You must become a true mermaid."

"Wait—what?" I tripped over a floating branch and lost my balance. Water soaked higher into my clothes before I managed to right myself. "Hang on a second. I can't just leave my family and join the mermaids. No offense—it sounds like a lot of fun, but . . ."

The Sweetwater Queen waved her tail slowly like a large fan. "We do not ask that you leave those you love. We ask only that you receive the ability to take our form."

"Couldn't I do that with the little shell she put in my hair?"

"That is temporary," said the Sweetwater Queen. "We wish you to know what it is to be one of us, that you may be our ally and advocate."

"I don't have to live under the sea? Or underground?"

"You must visit us from time to time, as our honored guest."

I glanced at Fisher. He nodded encouragement. "And you'll give me the Eye?" I said.

"It would be yours," she replied.

Having mermaid powers could certainly come in handy, and I liked my green-and-black tail a lot. Even if transforming was something I could only do in secret, it would still be the gift of a lifetime. Seriously—who *wouldn't* want to be a mermaid?

I touched the pearl on my necklace. "I'll do it."

"Ah, water witch. You'll not regret it," said the Saltwater Queen.

The Sweetwater Queen beckoned.

In for a penny, in for a gold coin. I splashed forward and sat in the water before the two mermaids. They gripped my shoulders and helped lower me the rest of the way down until I floated between them. The moon and stars lit the sky above me. "You're not going to drown me, right?" I joked, sort of.

They ignored me and began singing a strange harmony. The Sweetwater Queen's voice lilted over the rougher-edged sound of her companion's. As they sang, threads of blue and green magic criss-crossed my body, then sank onto my skin with a light stinging sensation.

When one of them seized my shoulders and the other my ankles, I realized they were about to push me under. My eyes shut and my lips pressed together just in time. Cold brackish water washed over me in waves, raising goosebumps.

I waited calmly, holding my breath, trusting they knew what they were doing and would not actually drown me. An uncontrollable tremor shot through my legs like I'd been woken from a dream of falling. All at once, I could *feel* the reality of both states of being—I had legs, yes—but hidden within, I now carried the power to become the black-and-green-tailed mermaid I had always been in my heart.

29

The merpeople swam away under the wavering phosphorescence. I watched them go, then retraced my steps from the cove to the walkway leading back to the marina and the hotel. There were more boats in the marina than there had been before.

I summoned Clove so I didn't feel so alone on the twisting, dimly lit path. She hopped alongside me, peeping and chirping when something caught her interest. More than once, she stopped to poke her nose into an interesting flower, or to half-climb a bit of garden statuary.

We rounded the corner to a raised overlook with a view of the sea, the bay, and the marina. A man stood facing the bay with some kind of fancy camera.

The strap on one of my athletic sandals was starting to chafe, so I paused at the overlook to put my foot on the railing and fix it. I was well within screaming distance of the pool area, so I wasn't too worried about the guy with the camera.

"Did you see the bioluminescence?" he said.

"Hm?" I glanced up briefly. "Oh. Yes, I did. Cool, huh?"

"It's like magic," he said. His camera shutter clicked, and clicked again. "Hard to capture."

Clove retreated behind me.

The man lowered the camera from its shooting position and turned to face me. The garden lights illuminated his face, which had just enough of a smile to show he had somehow amused himself with his own words. Not a bad-looking guy at all. Forty-ish, well-groomed.

But something about his eyes made me hurry to replace the strap and straighten up.

"Have a nice night," he called as I retreated to the path.

I walked quickly and rubbed my upper arms as if to remove a chill. When I got to the pool area, even the sparse late-night crowd was enough to make me feel relief at having other people around.

I pulled up a chair to the edge of the far side of the pool, away from the swimmers. Clove happily galloped across the pool deck and dove into the water. Her wet fur shone in the pool lights when she broke the surface.

"Best vacation ever." I had to laugh. I'd spent our vacation eating pancakes, chasing mermaids, sailing in the bay, soothing a mythical sea beast, committing petty theft of the neighbors' yard sign, and kissing my husband a lot more than usual, but now the vacation was almost over. Real life, with kids and jobs and laundry, hovered just outside the hotel gates—and so did the threat of Robert Wickham's witch list. How would it all fit together now?

I got up and trailed my fingers in the water. Clove swam over and nudged my hand affectionately. "'Night, Clove baby."

I left Clove swimming, and headed upstairs. Back in the room, I found Pete sprawled on the king bed, scrolling through his phone. "I've been looking into this Robert Wickham guy." He continued to scroll without looking up. "He seems to bounce around from Miami to the Bahamas."

"Any updates on the regatta?"

"Only the society column that said he was bringing his boat north."

I dropped onto the bed beside Pete and peered at the photo on his screen. "Is that his boat? The *Sundew*? Pretty name for a bad guy boat."

"Sundews are carnivorous plants."

"Oh." I leaned closer. "Can you zoom in on him?"

Pete adjusted the screen.

"Wait . . ." I said. "You're sure this is him?"

"Sure, I'm sure. See for yourself." He pulled up another, clearer photo from the search results, and handed me the phone.

I bolted up. "Pete—he's *here*. I saw him just now, down on the walkway. His clothes are different, his hair's a little different, but I wouldn't forget those eyes, not in a million years. What the hell is he doing at the Vivacqua? I thought he wasn't going to be here for another day!"

"Maybe he's using this marina for the *Sundew*?" He peered at the photo. "You need to let your friends know."

"Right. Right." I handed his phone back and grabbed my own. "What should I say? I can't reveal anything by phone; that's one of the rules."

"Just say 'He's here.'"

I typed the words, then erased them. "I can't. I can't leave a trail when we're about to pull several possibly illegal stunts." I shuddered. "How am I supposed to sleep tonight, knowing he's prowling around the hotel?"

"Which of your friends is up at this hour?"

"Nobody. Well, maybe Rose."

"Call Rose, then."

"I guess a call is better than putting it in a text." I hit the dial button. It rang a few times before Rose picked up. "Rose, it's me. He's here. What do I do?"

"He's *there?*"

"Yes!"

"Hang on."

Rose and Oliver's muffled voices carried over the line, but I couldn't hear what they were saying. Rose picked up again. "Oliver says he's coming out there."

"What should Pete and I do? Should we stay? Or should we go home?" I paced. "Is that worse, though? Then we'll just be stuck at home wondering where this guy is."

Another muffled exchange before Rose came back on. "He says it's probably better if you keep your family at a distance."

I glanced at Pete. He was far enough away that he couldn't have overheard. "Okay. I'll let you know." I hung up.

"What did Rose say?"

"Oliver's coming out to keep an eye on Wickham."

"And? What should we do?"

I agreed with Oliver. My family should be kept away. That meant Pete, Rocky, and Kevin.

But not me.

"Tomorrow morning, you pick up the kids like normal and take them home. They're fine where they are for tonight."

"And us?"

"What's he gonna do, grab me out of our hotel room?" I sounded cockier than I felt, but I wasn't giving up my pancake breakfast like some kind of chicken. "After that, if you can watch the kids, I will go take this guy out."

"You want me to watch the boys while you attack some witch hunter all by yourself."

"What, you think I can't handle it?"

"No, of course you can handle it. I just wish I could help."

"Watching the boys *is* helping. And I won't be by myself. There's Luella, and Rose, and Queenie, and Luella's mom, and Oliver, and—"

He threw his hands up and laughed. "All right, all right. You made your point."

I moved to the window. The outdoor lights pricked the garden around the aquamarine pool. The waterfalls had been turned off for the night. Beyond the hotel grounds, moonlight scattered on the bay and the ocean. "I hate that he's just wandering around down there, unsupervised. I mean, this is my vacation. It's practically my hotel. What right does he have to be here? I feel like someone should keep an eye on him till Oliver gets here."

Pete looked at me over the tops of his glasses. "I know what you're thinking, and it's a bad idea."

I crossed the room and smoothed my hands over his shoulders. "Not if you're with me. I'll be safe then."

"I think it's the other way around. If anyone ends up needing protection, it'll probably be me."

"But you always are so smart, and have such good ideas." I stroked his cheek. "I bet if we work together we can keep track of Robert Wickham and maybe even get some intel before Oliver gets here. You said you wanted to be involved . . ."

He closed his eyes and pressed his cheek into my touch. "Mm."

"And after Oliver gets here, we can come back upstairs."

He opened his eyes. "Mm?"

I wiggled my eyebrows up and down.

He promptly stood up and grabbed my hand. "Let's go."

30

The large Buddha statue in the garden provided great cover. We peeked out from behind its generous belly to get a view of the garden pathways twisting into the shadows.

"See anything?" I said.

"No, you?"

I shook my head.

We crept forward, our footsteps sounding louder than they had during the day. A night breeze shook the oak and palm branches overhead. We continued at a more normal pace down the path toward the marina.

"This would kind of be romantic if it wasn't also creepy," said Pete.

"This is why people go to horror movies on dates." I paused. "I hear something."

The faint sound of a whistle carried on the air.

"Do we hide?"

Camera Guy, AKA Robert Wickham, hadn't struck me as the whistling type. "No. Just act normal."

We kept strolling.

Flashlight illumination whipped across the sidewalk in front of me, then up into my eyes. "Hey! What's the big idea?"

The light went down, leaving bright afterimages in my vision.

"Sorry, ma'am," a masculine Southern voice drawled.

When my sight cleared, I saw the jokester security guard holstering his flashlight.

"I've seen you all before," he said. "You're the honeymooners."

I threw an arm around Pete's waist. "Yup, that's us. Honeymooning it up."

Then the guard peered at me more closely. "Weren't you on the minigolf course the other day?"

Uh-oh.

His forehead wrinkled like he was thinking hard enough to cause a headache. "I saw you and two other ladies down there running like the devil himself was after you."

Pete draped his arm over my shoulders. "What are you implying about my wife, sir?" he asked mildly.

The guard lifted his hands. "I don't mean no implication at all. It's just . . ." He leaned in. "I saw a man who was not your husband taking some pictures of you all."

Pete and I shared a brief, horrified look.

"What do you mean, *pictures*?" I said.

"At first I thought he might be a friend of yours. But when none of you went to talk to him, I realized he might not be. So I went to ask him what he was doing. By the time

I got over to where I'd seen him, he was gone. I mean, he might have just been taking pictures of the minigolf course and so on, but he seemed to be aiming in your direction."

"Have you seen him around since then?"

"No, ma'am."

I let go of Pete and dug in my purse. I found a Monaco Family Dental pen and an old receipt from Fifi's Secondhand Salon. I scribbled my number on the back of the receipt. "Here," I said, handing him the scrap. "If you see him around again, will you let me know?"

He took the paper and held it with both hands before folding it carefully and sliding it into his shirt pocket. Then he nodded. "You all have a nice night."

We wished him the same, and walked on.

"Ew, gross. Camera Guy is a creeper," I said, as soon as we were out of earshot.

"Let's see if we can find his boat," said Pete.

"And his camera, so I can smash it into bits and pieces."

We followed the path the rest of the way down to the bay.

The marina remained well-lit at night, a serious disadvantage to sneaking around. Every dock lay open to full view from the surrounding boats and to anyone at either end of the dock itself. I frowned. "There's no way to get close without being spotted."

"What if I went down there? You think he would recognize me?" Pete asked.

"If he's been taking pictures of Rose and Luella and me, who knows who else is on his radar?"

My phone blasted out the beginning of "Misirlou" at a decibel level that would have stunned an alligator. "Crap!" I fumbled for it and mashed the button to pick up while Pete and I retreated from the marina. "Hello?"

"I'm here," said Oliver. "Where are you?"

"At the marina. We'll meet you by the pool in a minute." I hung up and carefully toggled the ringer to vibrate. "What if I used the Key of Shadows like we did at the neighbors' house?"

Pete paused to consider. "You could sneak around that way, but if you popped back into reality out of thin air, you'd probably attract a lot more attention than sneaking around normally."

If Lenore had managed to steal an artifact from a museum and break into a skyscraper, why couldn't I figure out how to get closer to Robert Wickham?

I grabbed Pete's arm. "Wait—I know! We may not be able to see Robert Wickham himself, but we can explore his boat all we want."

"Right now?"

"Yes, right now, when did you think would be good? Next week? Come on!"

"What about Oliver?"

Now that I had an idea, I was itching to get going. "Go meet him and bring him up to date. I'll join you in fifteen minutes."

"You want to go *alone*?"

"I'll be fine. I'll be in and out. This is my thing, remember?"

"I thought this was Lenore's thing . . ."

"If Lenore can do it, I can do it."

"You're sure you won't—"

"Go!" I gave him a mostly playful shove.

When he had gone up the path and out of sight, I hurried to the nearest large statue—a bronze cow eating blades of metal grass—and ducked behind it. Having the Key of Shadows was kind of like being Clark Kent and needing to find a phone booth every so often.

I checked to make sure the Key was in contact with my skin. Then I imagined the shadow world, and crossed over instantly. Instead of near-midnight darkness, the sky lit up with filtered white light, kind of like an overcast day when a cold front is passing through. I could walk freely with no worries about running into anyone, so I quickly made my way down to the docks.

The bay water lay eerily still beneath the boats. Unlike when we had gone out on the *Tranquil Holiday*, there were no cheerful seagull calls to break the silence.

It took several false starts down various docks before I found the *Sundew*. The boat would have dwarfed the *Tranquil Holiday* if they were side by side. It made the little Hobie Cats look like mosquitoes, and it was even stranger to see their usually rainbow-hued sails striped in shades of gray.

A set of stairs attached to the dock led to the outdeck on the stern. Stairs on the boat led upward from the outdeck to an open dinette area with a wet bar. A set of what appeared to be automatic sliding doors didn't move when I approached, but slid open easily using the chrome handles.

Inside the salon, wraparound couches and a ten-person dining table filled the space, and another granite-topped wet bar ran along the port side.

I ran my hand over the cold stone. It would take a ridiculous amount of money to afford something like this—and if you were a rich person used to having everything done for you, it would be pretty unlikely to try to run it yourself. I mean, you could captain it yourself, and make your own meals, and do your own cleaning, but if you were going to drop your coins on a yacht of this level, you probably had, at minimum, a captain and a host or hostess to do the cooking and cleaning.

So Robert Wickham was probably not alone.

I continued in search of the master stateroom. They were usually forward, with the best view, or down low, in the most stable, quiet area of the boat, depending on the model. The chilly air, or maybe the absolute silence, made goosebumps prickle on my skin.

Three steps up led to a solid door, different from the sliding doors on the salon.

Sneaking around on my neighbor's lawn to steal a yard sign was one thing. Breaking into a multimillion-dollar yacht was another. But this guy deserved it.

I turned the handle, and the door swung open.

The carpet was so thick you hardly needed a bed to sleep on. The bed, however, dominated the space, with its pillows propped just so. No way he didn't have a housekeeper on board.

Broad windows offered an unobstructed view of the outside. Fresh roses sat in an oversized vase. Like everything else, they were gray.

I tugged one free and held it up to my nose. No scent at all.

I shook my head. I'd told Pete I would join him in fifteen minutes. I needed to get a move on and not stop to smell the flowers. I dropped the scentless gray rose and pulled open all the cubbies I could find. There was nothing in them but clothing, if there was anything at all. Most of them were empty. The closet held a boring assortment of dress shirts and pressed slacks. This guy wasn't a pack rat. In fact, his room was so clean it was a little weird.

The bedside table drawers were the only place I hadn't looked. I pulled open the nearest one.

Empty.

I flopped across the big bed to reach the other one. It slid open easily, revealing the dark velvet back of a heavy, ornate silver photo frame face-down in the drawer. I drew it out and flipped it over.

Robert Wickham, smiling in a suit—and a bride beside him, all in white.

31

Who leaves their wedding photo face-down in a drawer? Not a happily married person. Maybe he was cheating on her in his big fancy boat. Or maybe she'd left him and he could only tolerate the memories in small doses.

Whatever it was, I needed that photo. Every bit of information was another clue to taking him down.

Considering how the Key of Shadows had worked before, I couldn't simply grab the photo and take it with me. It would disappear like my shirt had in the garage.

Maybe I could take a picture of it with my phone. I pulled my phone out of my purse.

The screen was black even though I'd never turned it off, and thumbing the power button did nothing.

Right. When Pete and I had our own shenanigans in the shadows, there weren't any lights or televisions working there, either. So, no electronics in the shadows.

It would be wildly dangerous to leave the shadows while on the yacht. What if he was right there in the room with me?

"Think, Pepper!" I said to myself. It was nice to hear a human voice, even if it was only mine.

The bed was still made. That meant he hadn't gone to bed yet, at least not as of when I entered the shadows. He might even still be wandering the hotel, although I couldn't be sure. As far as I could tell, the shadow world was like a snapshot of the real world.

That brought up an interesting question. If you entered the shadows while on or in an object that could move—like a boat—what would happen if you came out of the shadows and it was no longer there? Would you drop into the water where it had been?

And what if he did see me? He obviously already knew who I was, knew I was a witch, and didn't feel like he needed to be secretive about it. Not if he was taking pictures in public and striking up conversations on the hotel walkway.

I rolled off the bed and knelt next to the drawer that held the photo. By kneeling, I made myself less obvious. All I needed to do was appear, open the drawer, grab the photo, and disappear again. I could do that.

Should I grab it, though? Then he'd know it had been stolen. Better to take a photo. If I could remain undetected, that would be best.

I slung my purse cross-body to keep it out of the way, and readied my phone. My heart raced. "Here goes nothing," I said. I concentrated on the real world—on roses with color, and throw pillows in a shade other than gray—and made the silent transition.

A quick glance around the room revealed that I was alone. I blew out my breath and hastily pulled open the drawer. I leveled my phone, which was back on like it had never been off, flipped the picture over, and took the shot.

Not a moment too soon, either. I could hear voices down the hall from the stateroom. I pressed the Key against my chest and wished myself back into the shadow world.

"Go, go, go," I said to myself, standing up from beside the table. I didn't know if they planned to stay docked all night or take off, and I didn't want to be dropped in the drink if I could avoid it. I hurried out of the stateroom, through the salon, and down the outdeck to the dock. Up the walkway, I hid behind the cow statue and returned to the real world.

A peek over the cow's back revealed no one in sight. I stepped onto the walkway and continued upward to the pool area.

Pete and Oliver sat at a poolside table. They both stood as I approached.

My husband hugged me. "You had me worried," he said.

I gave him a squeeze, then released him. "I'm fine. Check this out." I pulled out my phone and showed them the picture.

"Who is that?" said Oliver.

"I don't know. But it was the only interesting thing in his room. He's apparently not big on personal belongings."

Oliver studied the photo. "No account books?"

"Nothing. Just clothing."

He handed back my phone. "How did you manage to take this picture?"

"I popped out of the shadows."

Oliver's eyebrows shot up. "You did what?"

Pete sent Oliver a warning glance along the lines of: *Don't do it, buddy, she'll have your head.*

"That was extremely dangerous," said Oliver.

Pete winced.

"Yeah, well, put any parent in a position where they're on some kind of hit list and watch how they react," I said.

Oliver acknowledged the statement with a polite nod. "It was a statement of fact, not a criticism. Although I would much prefer if you would allow me to take the risks, where possible. That's what I'm here for. In fact"—he pulled out his own phone—"I have a message for you. From Rose." He pressed a button.

Rose's voice came out of his phone. "Pepper, it's me. I know your first impulse will be to run off and do something crazy, so please listen. This is the last night of your vacation. Go get some rest. Let Oliver take over for now. We'll meet up tomorrow and make plans."

I laughed. "Too late! I already did something crazy." I held my hands up after seeing their expressions. "All right, all right. I'm done for the night. I promise. But tomorrow . . ."

"Tomorrow," said Oliver, "you may wreak all the havoc you wish."

I rolled my eyes. "I'm glad I have everyone's permission."

"I will keep an eye on the *Sundew*."

I nodded. As much as I wanted to feel like I had everything under control, I didn't. But with my friends to back me up, I'd make it. "Thanks, Oliver. Come on, Pete. Let's go 'rest.'"

As we walked away, Pete put his arm around me. I leaned my head on his shoulder.

"I know you're worried, Pep."

"I'm not worried."

"You haven't mentioned being hungry all night."

"What does that have to do with anything?"

"It's not like you."

"I've just been busy, that's all. How about dessert? I could do dessert." I patted my stomach like I was eager. I wasn't. I had no appetite at all.

Pete eyed me, doing that mental math where you decide whether your spouse is telling the truth, and, if not, whether it's worth it to call them on it. "How about that apple tart you mentioned?"

My stomach rumbled like it was waking up. "An apple tart does sound kind of good."

We got the tart to go and took it back up to the room, where we shared it at the table before the vanilla ice cream turned into vanilla sauce.

"I actually do feel a little better," I said.

Pete got up, cleared away the trash, and propped all the pillows at the head of the bed. He scooted to the middle and beckoned me over.

I scooted onto the bed and curled up, facing away from him, toward the windows.

Pete wrapped around me, big spoon-style, and smoothed back my curls.

"Pete?"

He remained quiet, simply waiting for me to continue.

"I'm scared."

He didn't need to ask why. He didn't even need to say anything. He just pulled me closer and held me tight.

32

Pete left the next morning to pick up the kids. Since his destination was in the opposite direction and an hour and a half from Sparkle Beach, Rose drove down to give me a ride to Luella's. I hopped in her truck and slammed the door. "Let's go."

"Someone's had their coffee this morning."

"I had them put an extra shot of espresso in it."

"You never drink espresso."

"Today I do."

Rose revved the engine and put the truck in gear. "Check out the cup in the console."

I grabbed the Rolling Wave cruiser cup. It felt empty, but something rattled in the bottom. I pulled off the lid.

Inside, a brooch-sized piece of jewelry stared up at me. Literally.

The Eye of the Elements.

"Fisher brought it to Queenie for you," said Rose. "I put it in there for safekeeping until we got to Luella's. Also, you should know that Lenore's coming."

"Lenore? Why?"

"Because she's the one with the most experience with the Eye."

I made a face.

"I know. But if we're going to use it, she could be a big help."

"Or she could steal it and disappear," I said.

"That, too. But she's also volunteered to be our guinea pig."

The towering hotel building shrank behind us as we crossed the bridge and turned north toward Sparkle Beach. The next highway exit led east, past Highway to Grill, across River Street, and over the downtown bridge, to Luella's cozy shotgun house on Seabreeze Lane.

I grabbed the cruiser cup, got out, bounded up the porch stairs, and knocked on the door. "Luella, it's us."

The door opened to reveal Luella in her comfy clothes—capri pants and colorful top—and her hair pulled back for business. "Come on in, y'all. I was just about to lay out the refreshments."

Lenore was sitting on the couch. She eyed me up and down. "I hear you've been using my key."

"Hilda's key," corrected Rose.

Lenore sent her a withering look. "She gave it to me, didn't she?"

Luella reappeared with a big plate piled high with her special cowboy cookies. "Who likes cookies?" she said, with probably a little more emphasis than normal. She laid the plate on the coffee table and took a seat on the other end of the couch from Lenore.

Rose took a spare chair.

I sat on the floor.

"So, tell me what mischief you've been up to," said Lenore.

I hesitated. I didn't love bringing Lenore in on this, but I also didn't love not having a solution to the Robert Wickham problem.

Then I told her everything, from stealing a sign to snapping the picture on the yacht.

She raised an eyebrow. "Good thing he didn't move that yacht around while you were in the shadows."

"Why?" asked Luella.

"Think about it," said Lenore. "Let's say you enter the shadows and walk to a busy intersection. While you're in the shadows, nothing moves. Electricity doesn't work. The cars just sit there. But if you suddenly popped back into real life . . ." She smacked her hands together so hard the noise echoed. "That's why you have to be careful where you enter and exit the shadows. In your case you probably would have just fallen in the water, but still."

Calamity-filled images of cars, boats, trains, and airplanes filled my mind in rapid succession. "Ouch. And I still didn't get anything good."

"Don't discount yourself," said Luella. "Just because you didn't find something right away, doesn't mean he isn't hiding something somewhere we don't know about."

"How are we supposed to get at that?" I said. I pointed a warning finger at Lenore. "Don't say 'Kidnap him.'"

Lenore smiled.

"Mrs. Millefleur said we might try mind-reading," said Luella.

"Right," said Rose, "but how would we get Mrs. Millefleur in the same room as Robert Wickham?"

I snapped my fingers. "The regatta! She's a prominent local business leader—she'll practically be expected to be there!"

Lenore waved a hand dismissively. "Not enough. They'd have to be face-to-face. Eye to eye. If her name's on his list, he already knows who she is. He's not going to stand around and wait for her to read his mind. Same for your friend." She gestured to Rose.

"Kidnapping is sounding better," I said.

"Is there anyone he would *tell* the information to?" said Rose. "Voluntarily?"

"I doubt it. He's like some kind of ultra-rich loner. There was literally nothing in his room except the wedding photo. And—on top of that—he and his wife don't seem to be together anymore. Pete and I tried to find more pictures online, but they were all old. They haven't been photographed together in months. Possibly longer."

"So much for that," said Lenore.

Luella frowned. "If he'd recognize most of us, how are we supposed to do anything?"

"What if someone unexpected talked to him?" I said.

The three of them looked at me.

"Who?" said Rose.

"His wife."

Lenore laughed and shook her head. "Where are you going to dig her up?"

"What if I didn't need to? What if I could just *look* like her? I could keep him talking long enough to read his mind."

"But you can't read minds," said Luella.

"No, but Rose and Mrs. Millefleur can." I lifted the cruiser cup. "Maybe with a boost, they can do it from a distance."

Luella and Lenore looked completely confused.

I pulled off the lid and showed them the Eye. "Ta-da! Rose and Mrs. Millefleur can load it up with mind-reading juice."

Rose made a skeptical face. "Okay, let's assume that we can read his mind with the help of the artifact's extra power. How on earth would you disguise yourself as his wife? I mean, you both have curly hair and similar skin tone, but that's where the resemblance ends. There's no way he would mistake you for her."

"Maybe there is a way," said Luella. "Mama told me one time that if you combined all the elements just right, you could make an illusion."

Rose nodded slowly. "'Water of the blood, fire of the mind, earth of the body, air between all.'"

"You realize how creepy that sounds, right?" said Lenore, taking another cookie. "Water and blood and bodies?"

"Hush," said Luella. "You weren't there."

"I'm kind of glad I wasn't."

"We have fire, air, and water here," I said, gesturing to Rose, Luella, and myself. "No earth."

"You might, though," said Lenore. "In the Eye. I hardly used any earth magic. Only fire, air—and water, by accident."

I peered at the jeweled Eye. "I don't want to blow anyone's face off by experimenting."

"Don't use it on some*one*. Use it on some*thing*," said Lenore.

"How?" I said.

Luella dusted cookie crumbs from her hands. "If I recall correctly, water is the base of the illusion. Earth is the substance of it. Fire animates it, and air is the linking force."

"So, like, tiny water droplets?" I said.

Luella nodded. "And tiny bits of earth."

"This seems complicated," said Lenore. "Just throw him in the shadows."

"That's Plan B," I said. "We're not there yet."

Rose held up a cookie. "Here's a simple one. Can we make an oatmeal cookie look like a Christmas cookie?"

"I'm game," I said, "but who's going to run the artifact so we have some earth power in the mix?"

Rose, Luella, and I looked at each other before our gazes shifted, reluctantly, to Lenore.

She raised an eyebrow. "Aren't you worried I'll knock you out and run off with it?"

"Yes," said Rose.

"Maybe we should wait," said Luella.

"I'm not waiting. Give me your phone, Lenore."

"Why?"

"Just do it." I pocketed the Eye to free my hands.

She frowned, but tugged her tiny phone from her pocket and handed it over.

I opened the contacts. There was only one. I copied the number into a note on my own phone.

"What are you doing?" she said.

"I'm setting up an electronic dead man's switch." I handed Lenore her phone back, then typed rapidly on my phone keyboard. "This text message I'm typing about the museum theft, with your name and your son's phone number, will be sent instantly to the Miami Police Department tip line—"

Lenore jumped up. "*What?*"

I stepped back in case she tried to lunge at me across the coffee table. "*If* I don't put in the code to cancel it within one hour." I pressed the button to finalize.

"You—you—" Lenore sputtered.

Rose cracked up.

"She got you good," said Luella.

I set my phone on the coffee table and pulled the Eye out of my pocket. "Ready to play nice?'

Lenore's glare melted into an amused look. "I knew I liked you. Give me the damn artifact." She held out her hand.

Even with the fail-safe in place, I couldn't help hesitating before I handed it over.

33

Rose covered her face with her hands. "We've been at this for half an hour, and our 'Christmas cookie' *still* looks like a lump of diseased clay."

I punched a pillow on the couch and flopped down. "At this rate, my face is going to look like a Picasso painting."

"Is it the artifact?" said Luella. "Is it not strong enough?"

Rose shook her head. "It's us. We can't picture what we want accurately enough."

"Hey, I never claimed to be a cookie artist," said Lenore. "Knowing what a cookie should look like doesn't necessarily mean you can draw one."

Each of us picked up one of the remaining four cookies. We ate them in silence. Luella, Rose, and Lenore appeared to be thinking hard. I was thinking, too. There had to be a solution.

"An artist!" I slapped my forehead. "We need Raphael. He can control the look of the illusion."

Luella seized me in a quick hug, showering me with cookie crumbs in the process. "Of course! Why didn't I think of that? We'll power it, he'll make it look pretty. I'll text him right now."

"On to the next problem," said Rose. "Even if we master this illusion, it's too small to cover Pepper's whole body. The best we can do is change the look of her face and hair. What do we do with the rest of her?"

Luella, Lenore, and Rose looked me up and down.

"What dresses do you own, Pepper?" asked Luella.

"Dresses?" I laughed. "Try 'none.'" Then I caught the look on Luella's face. The look that said *shopping trip*. "Oh, no. Not another makeover. Why does every grand plan have to end with me getting dressed up?"

"Because," said Luella, with Southern delicacy, "khaki shorts and comfy t-shirts do not a regatta make."

I stuck out my tongue at her.

"Third problem," said Rose. "We want to make this guy look like nothing he says can be trusted. We said we'd do that by making Oliver's bear attack him in front of the regatta crowd. How are we going to make him see a familiar?"

"That's where I come in." Lenore slid the Eye of the Elements across the coffee table. "Practice on me."

I scooped up the Eye and cancelled the automatic text message I'd used to ensure her good behavior.

"But if Lenore already kind of *wants* to see our familiars, how will practicing on her help with making Robert Wickham see a familiar?" asked Luella.

236

"Don't you see?" I said. "Robert Wickham's no different. He's spent all this time trying to find magic. He *wants* to find it. That's all Rose needs—the desire." I glanced at Rose, who nodded. "He just won't realize that the bear attacking him is magic—at least, not until later, when he's had time to calm down and think it over."

Lenore shook her head. "You can't just throw a bear at him and expect him to swallow it. You need to soften him up."

"And how would we do that?" said Rose.

"What've you got?"

Rose blinked. "Got?"

"Familiars," said Lenore.

"Oh. A bear, a raccoon, a dog, a cat, an otter, a squirrel, and a crow."

"Start with the dog. A rabid dog's believable. Then you hit him with the others. Then, when he's in a complete panic, you send in the bear."

"That's . . . actually not a bad idea," said Rose. "Let's practice." She got up and pulled a stool out from the small bar separating the kitchen from the living room. "Sit here, facing the kitchen. I won't be able to make eye contact with Robert Wickham, so I don't want to be able to see your eyes, either."

Lenore went to the bar and sat on the stool, rotating herself away from the living room.

We summoned our familiars. Zephyr's fluffy white tail waved as she greeted Horatio with a friendly sniff. Clove hopped in circles before going nose-to-nose with

Horatio, who backpedaled as if his personal space had been intruded on.

Horatio shook out his front paws and gave Clove a wide berth on his way to the kitchen. He sprang to the kitchen counter and sat facing Lenore, his tail twitching.

"Can you see anything?" I said to Lenore.

"Am I supposed to see something?"

"Not yet," said Rose. "Hang on." Concentration tightened her face. "How about now?"

"Nope," said Lenore.

Rose's hands balled into fists. "Now?"

Lenore spun around and regarded Rose. "If you keep tensing up like that, you'll explode."

Rose exhaled and dropped onto the couch.

Luella sat next to her. "It's only the first try."

"Here." I offered Rose the amulet. "Charge it up a little. Then you can use the stored magic along with your magic."

Rose cradled the Eye of the Elements in her hands. Silver magic trickled over it and disappeared into the tiny jeweled pupil. "I don't want to overdo it. I can't exhaust myself before tomorrow."

"Just enough to see if it works," I said.

Rose sighed and stood up. She clasped the Eye in her hands and faced Lenore. This time, she closed her eyes. Instead of tensing, she tipped her head back and breathed slowly and deeply. Tiny silver points of light spilled from her hands like airborne glitter.

The silver magic floated to Lenore and settled over her head and shoulders.

Lenore straightened up. "Oh—look at the little kitty cat man!"

Horatio blinked his golden eyes.

"Go, Zephyr!" said Luella.

Zephyr bounded into the air and hovered in the kitchen near Horatio.

Lenore nearly fell off the stool. She struck the bar and laughed. "I'll be damned."

"One more," I said. "Go, Clove, go!"

Clove scurried over to Lenore and went on her hind legs like she was begging for a treat. She chirped until Lenore finally looked down and did a double take.

Rose grimaced. "I can't hold it much longer."

"Let it go," said Luella.

Rose exhaled and sat. She let her head fall back against the couch. "That was intense. I'm going to need to charge this thing a little bit at a time tonight if it's going to be ready for tomorrow. How long do you think I'll need to make the familiars visible?"

"Three or four minutes?" I said. "Enough time for him to freak out and people to take notice."

"I'll aim for five," she said.

Since we didn't want to tire Rose out, and we weren't mastering the illusion magic with Raphael, we decided to pause for the moment. We piled into Luella's sedan and dropped Lenore off at Mrs. Millefleur's beachside mansion before heading downtown to Fifi's Secondhand Salon.

Fifi, the big black poodle who served as the store's mascot, greeted us when the door jingled open. The turbaned owner looked up from the cash wrap. "Will it be hair or flair today, ladies?"

"Flair," I said.

"Anything in particular?"

"Just browsing," said Luella.

We entered the consignment store side.

"What am I supposed to wear for this?" I said.

Luella was already sliding dress hangers. "Look up the wife and see what she used to wear to formal events."

I entered the name "Jane Wickham" into a search engine.

Rose looked over my shoulder as I scrolled through pictures. "She wears a lot of black, but it's not really goth," she said. She stopped my scroll. "See the gloves? Between those and her hair all piled up like that, there's a *Desperately Seeking Susan* vibe going on."

I shrugged. "She just looks like a deer in the headlights to me."

Luella huddled with us. "Let me see." She nodded as I scrolled through the old society page pictures. "Rose is right. *Desperately Seeking Susan*, but on a champagne budget. Give me a sec." She returned to the racks and rifled through several sections. She pulled out several short black dresses and tiny jackets.

Rose went to the cash register and asked for the tray of gloves.

This was not looking good. "You guys, I can't pull off a bunch of weird lace and fingerless gloves and . . . good God, Luella, I'm not wearing that dress!"

Luella smoothed her hand down a black cocktail dress that barely reached her thighs.

I scoffed. "You can't tell me that's what people wear to regattas."

"No, but according to the pictures, it's what Jane Wickham wore *everywhere*. Charity galas, ribbon-cuttings, you name it."

"Is anyone wondering what they saw in each other? I mean, he's a slick corporate type. She's some edgy-looking chick." Rose paused. "Never mind. I just answered my own question."

Luella held the first dress out to me. "Put it on—and make sure it covers up your tattoo."

34

When I finally got dropped off at home, it took both hands to wrestle all the bags up the driveway.

So far, the neighbors hadn't replaced their awful sign yet. Let them try it. Because if they did, it would be gone overnight.

I bumped my foot against the front door in hopes that someone would hear and unlock it for me.

Voices and a stampede of footsteps carried from inside.

"Mom! Mom!" Kevin flung open the door so hard it slammed into the wall. "No soup for you!" he shouted. Then he threw his arms around my waist.

I dropped the bags and hugged him tight. "How's my bestest boy?"

Rocky stepped closer and cleared his throat.

"And my other bestest boy! Get in here!" I grabbed him and pulled him in.

Pete leaned against the wall and tilted his head. "What about me? Am I the bestest, too?"

I laughed and released the kids. They ran off down the hall.

Pete came close. I rested my head on his chest. When he spoke, the words quietly rumbled through me. "How did it go?"

"Fine." I closed my eyes.

"Want to talk about it?"

"Nope."

"Want to go for a swim?"

I lifted my head. "Now that sounds like a plan. Give me a minute to put my stuff away and get changed."

"Boys, we're going swimming," called Pete.

Answering whoops came from Kevin and Rocky.

Before I could gather up the bags again, Pete stopped me. "Wait," he said. "I have something to show you." He beckoned me down the hall, then opened Kevin's bedroom door oh-so-slowly to reveal . . .

A perfectly clean floor. Not a Lego in sight.

I gasped. "You didn't."

"I did. With a little help from our 'heirs.' Figured you had enough on your plate right now."

Kevin burst in. "Hey, people! I gotta get changed." He shooed us out and shut the door.

Pete and I shared an amused look.

I gathered up the bags and took them to the master bedroom, where I emptied all of them on the bed. Dress, shoes, accessories, even hairstyling supplies to make my curls look more like Jane Wickham's. Anything to further the illusion.

I stowed away the accessories and set the shoes on the floor. The hair products I placed on the bathroom counter. The dress I held up in the mirror. Too short, too black, and too fancy for my taste. Why couldn't Jane Wickham have the decency to enjoy cargo shorts and comfy t-shirts like a normal person?

I stuck my tongue out at my reflection before hanging the dress on the back of the bathroom door to knock out wrinkles. Then I changed into my bathing suit, grabbed a few towels, and headed to the pool.

The boys—all three of them—were already outside.

Kevin made a leap for the deep end. "Cannonball!" Water fountained upward and landed on the pool deck with a noisy splatter.

Rocky used the steps and waded into the shallow end. Pete followed him in.

It didn't feel right to play in the water without Clove, but I couldn't risk calling for her out loud, even quietly, so instead I just pictured her little face with its silver whiskers.

She leaped out of the pool in a burst of real water and a silvery spray of magic. She ran over, galloped around my feet, then bunched up beside me like a furry brown spring, facing the pool.

I knew what she wanted. "Move, Kevin," I said.

He swam easily out of the way.

I stepped my foot back like a runner doing a standing start, then took two quick steps and a leap. "Cannonball!"

Clove launched beside me, and we hit the water together.

Underwater, I held my breath, waiting for the descent to stop and the bubbles to clear. I unfolded my legs and pushed off from the bottom. When I broke the surface, I dipped my head backward to slick my hair away from my face.

Clove was still swimming loop-the-loops below.

"Way to go, Mom!" said Rocky.

I smiled. Wouldn't it be fun if my kids could see Clove, too?

Honestly, it was too big of a secret to put on them at this age. They'd probably go tell their friends—or worse, their teachers. Luella's mom had waited until Luella was in her *forties* to tell her. I didn't want to wait that long, but right now they were still too young.

"Splash fight!" said Kevin. He aimed wild splashes at the rest of us. Most of them missed. He had more enthusiasm than aim.

I splashed him back. "Of course you know this means war!"

Rocky shielded his face with one arm and splashed with the other.

Clove surfaced, took one look at the chaos, and dove back under. Likewise, Pete retreated to the far corner of the pool and draped his arms over the side.

After we had splashed ourselves out, we played a few rounds of Marco Polo. Then I got the rainbow-colored diving sticks out and tossed them at random throughout the pool. Kevin and Rocky dove down to bring them up.

Clove, apparently, wanted to be helpful. She dove down, grabbed one in her paws, and swam to me, dropping it at my feet. Luckily, the kids were too busy diving to notice the mysteriously mobile diving stick.

Since we hadn't had a chance to restock the fridge yet, we ordered pizza for dinner. Pete and the kids ate it by the pool while the setting sun silhouetted the backyard palm trees. Clove leaped out of the pool, hid behind a big potted plant to shake off excess water, and then hopped over to the table—presumably in hopes of falling pepperoni slices.

I wanted to eat, too, but my stomach turned on me. Too many worries to let my appetite run free.

I'd put some in the fridge for tomorrow.

Tomorrow, this would all be over.

I opened the sliding glass door to go inside. Clove hastily jumped up and ran to follow me. We slipped inside, and I took out my phone to call Luella. "Hey, it's me." I could hear other people in the background when she answered.

"Hey, Pep! You caught me on a break from practice. Raphael and Mama are here, plus Rose, Oliver, Queenie, Lenore, and Mrs. Millefleur. It's wild. I never thought I'd see the day." Luella laughed.

"Should I come over? Maybe I should practice more, too."

"Don't fret. We're just making sure everything goes smoothly. All you have to do tonight is relax."

"Relax," I said. "Right."

"Who's on the phone? Is that Pepper?" Mama's voice went from background noise to full volume. "Hey, girl! Don't you let me hear you're fretting yourself to death over there, or I might have to come over and give you what for."

The phone changed hands again. "Pepper, it's Rose. We got this. *You* got this."

Another rustle, and Luella spoke again. "Did you eat yet?"

"We ordered some pizza."

"Yeah, but did you eat any?"

"No."

"Well, then. Get yourself some slices, you hear me? Don't make me send Mama over there. You don't want that. She's feeling feisty."

"She's *always* feeling feisty."

"True. I gotta get back to practicing, now. We'll see you tomorrow at the regatta. You know where to go, right?"

I told her I did, and we hung up after saying goodnight. I had to smile to myself at the thought of all them squeezed into Luella's little house, trying to pull everything together before tomorrow.

Clove went on her hind legs and rested her front paws on my knee. She looked up at me as if she wanted me to know that everything would be okay. I bent low to run my hand over her sleek head and back.

Everything *would* be okay. It *had* to be.

I slid open the sliding glass door and stepped onto the pool deck.

Rocky jumped up from his seat and held out an open box of pizza. He beamed. "See? We didn't eat it all. We saved you some."

My kids, no matter how old they got or how boisterous they could be, were still the sweetest. They were the ones I was fighting for. And my friends were working overtime to make sure everything went to plan.

"Do it like this!" said Kevin. He folded his slice in half and took a big bite.

The scent of pepperoni filled my nose.

Maybe I could manage a slice after all.

35

I knocked at the double doors of the hotel suite Mrs. Millefleur had arranged to use as our temporary command center. Although I didn't usually have a problem with heights, this room was on an even higher floor than our room had been. Either the building itself was swaying slightly—or I was.

Luella pulled open the doors. "Pepper!"

I hoisted my bags and stepped across the threshold.

The marble entryway led past a mirror over a carved wooden table that held a large metal bowl. The entryway opened up to a great room with four large windows overlooking the ocean. Couches and a chaise lounge filled one side of the room. The other side was dominated by a long dining table. Raphael sat at the far end of the table, near the window. Queenie stood by the window, and Luella's mother sprawled comfortably on the chaise lounge. Mrs. Millefleur stood at the nearer end of the dining table with a map of the Vivacqua before her.

Queenie bustled over and air-kissed my cheeks. Then she took me firmly by the shoulders. "How are you feeling, darling? Are you nervous?"

I laughed. "Nervous? I'm not nervous. My middle name is 'Danger.'" I set the bags down and noticed that my hands were only slightly shaking. "What could go wrong?"

With a fancy hat pinned to her hair, Mrs. Millefleur looked like she might be on her way to meet the queen of England. The regatta's grand after-party was practically the whole point of the event, other than the actual sailboat races. "Does everyone understand what they are to do?"

"You've only explained it a hundred times," said Mama, from her spot on the suite's chaise lounge. Luella's mother smoothed her uncharacteristically demure powder-blue skirt and patted her own hat, a matching Jackie Onassis-style pillbox with two tiny feathers. "I ain't fixin' to wear these duds all day, you know."

Mrs. Millefleur pointedly ignored her. "Oliver is already downstairs in the crowd. He will communicate to Rose via the fire opal she is wearing"—she glanced at Rose, who gave her a thumbs up to confirm—"and let us know when Wickham makes an appearance. Pepper, of course, will take the fire opal before she joins the party as Jane Wickham. Raphael?"

He glanced up from the dining table, where he had been deeply absorbed in sketching something on a piece of paper.

"Are you ready?"

He held up the paper: a perfect pencil-drawn likeness of Jane Wickham. "Ready."

She nodded. "I will join the VIPs and make sure the press is in place at the proper time. The rest of you will come down one at a time so as not to attract attention, Pepper last of all. Anyone who is not currently casting a spell will keep a lookout for those of us who are."

"If anybody asks," said Mama, "just tell 'em we're praying. Nobody'll argue with that." She cackled.

"Mildy sacrilegious but not one of your worst ideas," said Mrs. Millefleur. "Pepper will speak to Wickham long enough for Rose and I to read his mind for the location of the accounting books. When we have all the information we need, we will release the familiars. Any questions?"

I waved. "Me! I have a question. I may *look* like Jane Wickham, but how do I *act* like Jane Wickham? What am I supposed to say to this guy?"

"You'll have to improvise, darling," said Queenie. "Go with the flow. You are a water witch, after all."

"Go with the flow," I repeated, in an attempt to psych myself up. "I can do that." I'd found one short video clip online that captured a few moments of her speech and mannerisms. It would have to be enough.

"It shouldn't take that long," Rose pointed out. "As soon as we have the information, you can retreat."

"And we're right there if anything should go wrong," said Luella.

I glanced around the room. "Where's Lenore?"

"At home, where she should be, considering that an appearance at such a public event would be unwise." Mrs. Millefleur met each person's gaze. "Anything else?"

No one spoke.

"Very well. I will go down first. Belinda, follow in five minutes. The rest of you when Rose hears from Oliver." She walked to the other end of the table and tapped Raphael's paper. "Burn this." Her heels clicked on the marble floor as she walked out.

Raphael lifted the portrait to the light. "Too bad. I kind of liked it."

Luella kissed him on top of his head. "It's lovely."

Rose flipped my bags upside down one by one. She scooped up the clothing and handed it to me with a meaningful look.

"All right, all right. I'm going. But this is the last time I'm dressing up for *anything*." I retreated to the suite's master bedroom and shut the door. Then I took off my t-shirt and shorts and shimmied into the little black dress. It didn't exactly go along with the regatta look, but if it was what Jane Wickham usually wore, that was what was important.

The worst thing was the shoes. I'd worn athletic sandals and tennis shoes for so long I was practically allergic to heels. At least these were chunky enough to provide some stability.

I clomped to the door and opened it. "I'm decent," I called.

Luella and Rose joined me and gave me a once-over.

"Let's fix your hair," said Luella, diplomatically. She steered me to a vanity table.

"And your makeup," added Rose.

Luella brushed out my curls to loosen them up, then pinned them to the top of my head in bird's nest fashion.

Rose had me turn the chair to face her. She flipped open a large tray of eyeshadow and went to work.

I resisted the urge to fidget. "Does it really have to take this long?"

"Jane Wickham favors a smoky eye. The more you resemble her, the easier it is to create the illusion. Sit still."

I sighed and let her keep piling the stuff on.

When Rose was finished, Luella layered on the costume jewelry and handed me a pair of fingerless gloves.

I shoved my hands into the gloves and stood up. "Well?" I spread my arms. "How do I look?"

"Like a mad punk rock fairy," said Rose.

"Are you sure this is right for a regatta?"

"It's what Jane wore all the time," said Luella with a shrug. "You saw the pictures."

I regarded my reflection. The cord for the Key of Shadows disappeared beneath the neckline of the dress. "Do you think she'll mind that I borrowed her face for the afternoon?"

Rose's gaze caught mine in the mirror. "I'm sure she would mind—if she knew about it."

Luella patted my shoulder. "It's for a good cause."

I twisted this way and that, looking at my appearance from all angles. "Don't get me wrong. I don't feel bad about doing this to *him*, but it is a little weird to wear someone's face like a Halloween costume." I posed with my gloved hands framing my messy up-do. "If I ever meet her, I'll tell her I'm sorry."

Rose's hand went to her fire opal pendant. "It's Oliver." She turned away. "You spotted him?" she said, speaking to

Oliver. Then she went quiet, listening to a response only she could hear.

Luella and I looked at each other.

"Got it," said Rose. "We'll get Pepper ready, then we'll come down." She released the pendant. "Wickham has come ashore from the *Sundew*."

"Showtime," said Luella.

I followed them out to the living room.

Queenie stepped forward and held out the Eye of the Elements. "You'll need this to focus Rose and Hilda's fire magic on him."

"Where do I put it?" I patted my nonexistent pockets.

"Can it go on the cord with the Key of Shadows?" asked Luella.

I tugged it out and threaded the open cord through the filigree around the Eye, then tied the cord tight again and tucked both artifacts into my dress. They were lumpy, but the lace around the neckline helped cover them up.

"And here's the fire opal," said Rose, unclasping the necklace and handing it over.

I reclasped it around my neck. "I feel like a walking artifact museum."

You are one, said Oliver.

In my head.

"Whoa! He can hear everything I say?"

Rose nodded. "He can think at you, but you can't think back at him. If you want him to hear you, you have to speak."

"Well, that's a relief." At least my thoughts were private.

Raphael laid down his pencil and joined us.

Queenie's gaze took in each of us. "Earth, air, fire, and water. All the elements are in place. Are you prepared, darlings, to take down this threat to all witches?" She took my hand and squeezed it.

I squeezed back. "Let's kick some butt."

They began the spell.

Rose, Luella, and Queenie channelled their magic to Raphael in swirls of silver. His graceful artist's hands swooped around my face, sculpting the magic into something I could neither see nor feel.

When the silver faded, they stared at me.

My gloved hands went to my face. "Did it work?"

Rose smirked. "It worked, all right."

Luella reached out and touched the end of my nose with one fingertip, gently, as if the illusion might pop like a soap bubble. "It's uncanny. But hold still—there's one more thing. You need to talk for a minute. Or sing."

"Who knew I'd be starring in *The Little Mermaid*?" I launched into the wordless melody Ariel sings while her voice is taken.

Luella's hands fluttered near my neck, sending up bright flashes of magic. "Done."

I hurried to the entryway mirror and examined myself. My fingers traced Jane's heart-shaped face and her pointed chin, her large, liquid eyes surrounded by a lake of eyeshadow. Even though I had her features, I didn't have the deer-in-the-headlights look she seemed to have in that photo.

Queenie appeared behind me in the reflection. "Remember, darling. It will last about one hour, so get to him as quickly as you can."

I shook out my hands and bounced on my heels to dispel some of the nervous energy that was flashing through me. "One hour. Got it." My voice sounded strange—brittle and cool—not my own at all.

Raphael handed Rose the portrait.

She lit the paper with a touch, tossed it in the metal bowl, and watched it burn.

36

We dispersed in the lobby so we didn't draw attention to ourselves as a group. The many garden paths meant we could each approach the party from a different angle.

I chose the one I'd taken on the night of the mermaid gift exchange.

Oliver's voice entered my mind without warning. *Pepper, can you hear me?*

"Yes," I said quietly. I didn't want to look like I was talking to myself, but there wasn't any other way to be heard.

Hang back for a moment, if you would. The others are getting into position.

"Okay." I stopped and fidgeted with my little black bag at the overlook. The sandwich baggies holding my emergency snack mix—double-bagged for freshness—were poking out from under the flap.

A large white tent filled part of the grassy area above the marina. Outside the tent, long tables with white tablecloths framed two sides of the lawn. Soft music wafted on the salty breeze along with the scent of champagne. Women and men wore pastel colors; I smoothed my hands over my black dress with a slight grimace. Rose and Luella had said this was the right outfit. I could only hope they had chosen correctly.

They are in place. Wickham is at the refreshments table to the east of the tent.

"On my way." This was it. I carefully walked down the remaining steps to the party.

I hoped I wouldn't run into anyone else who knew Jane. It seemed unlikely, but not impossible.

I grabbed a glass of champagne but only pretended to drink. The lipstick left impressions on the glass. Was it her lip print or mine? I couldn't tell.

Robert Wickham stood facing away from me in a navy blazer and light khaki pants, looking about as scary as your average church deacon. He threw his head back and laughed heartily at something someone else said, then followed this up with a sip from his champagne glass.

Strange to see this daytime version who seemed to be full of friendliness, versus the night I'd seen him with his camera, all creepy and calm.

"Are Rose and Mrs. Millefleur ready?" I murmured to Oliver.

They are ready, came his immediate reply.

All I had to do was keep this guy occupied while they ransacked his mind. Piece of cake.

How would his wife have approached him? I had no idea. Best to make him react. I made my way across the lawn, wobbling slightly on my heels, and tapped him on the shoulder.

He turned, all smiles and charm . . .

Until his gaze landed on me, dark and instantly cold.

I couldn't help but shiver, even as the reassuring sight of Rose and Mrs. Millefleur's combined magic trickled toward him.

His eyelids tightened as he forced a laugh. "Jane! What are you doing here?"

I knew they hadn't been photographed together in a while, but the bad blood seemed to be a little badder than I expected. I let out a light laugh of my own. "Oh, you know."

The magic sprinkled over his head like silver dandruff.

He gestured with his glass. "Everyone, this is my wife, Jane." Something about the way he said *wife* made my skin prickle.

I smiled and nodded at the small cluster of pastel-clad regatta fans. The less I said, the better.

"Jane has been leading me on quite the merry chase, haven't you, dear?"

Had I? I mean, had *she*? It was like one of those dreams where you're in a play and you're the only one who hasn't memorized their lines.

"Excuse us, won't you?" he said to his companions, who smiled and nodded back as if nothing was wrong. He took the glass right out of my hand and put it down on the table with his unfinished glass of champagne. Then he took my elbow.

It probably looked like an affectionate squeeze. It felt like a vise. He steered me away from the crowd so fast I nearly tripped. "Did you think you'd be safe here, Jane, with your little witch friends?" he hissed in my ear.

My heart nearly stopped. My witch friends? Did he *know* what was going on?

Wait—he had called me Jane. The illusion was working. He saw me as Jane, not Pepper. But what did he mean about *witch* friends? Why would *Jane* be friends with witches?

Unless—

"I would admire your audacity if it wasn't so colossally stupid. You ran from me once. I won't let it happen again. Not after you've been so helpful with my little project."

His fingers dug into my arm as he half-dragged me away from the party, toward the docks.

At least he hadn't noticed the fire magic burrowing into his skull.

If only I could have spoken to Oliver, or communicated with Rose and Luella, or any of the rest of our group! But no, I was on my own unless I bailed out. I couldn't bail out. I had to think.

Then it hit me.

Jane had witch friends—Jane could help him with his "project"—because *Jane* was a *witch*.

I stumbled and would have fallen but for his grip on my arm.

Jane Wickham was a witch. Her husband knew she was a witch. Maybe she'd told him too much, been his unwitting source before it all went wrong.

No wonder she had run.

Our footsteps rattled on the boards of the dock, and the *Sundew* came into view.

"I told you if you didn't do what I said, I'd expose all of them. And now it's come to that." He came to a sudden stop, still gripping my arm with one hand. "Unless—" His eyes searched mine. "Unless you came back to make peace." His free hand went to my jaw, tracing its contours before tilting my chin up. "To stop running."

I suppressed the urge to throw up on his expensive-looking shoes. Did he actually think she had come back to him? Arrogant freaking bastard. If I wasn't on a mission I'd have drowned him in the bay right then and there. Actually, Rose's powers seemed even more appealing. This guy deserved to be roasted, toasted, and burnt to a crisp.

I cast my gaze down to hide my feelings. "Yes," I said, all meekness with a touch of a pout. A quick glance at his triumphant sneer, and I didn't need to read minds to see that he thought he'd won.

His thumb brushed my lower lip. "You came to your senses."

Ugh. I kept my eyes down and nodded.

"Why don't we take a cruise and talk about it?"

Oliver's voice blazed through my head: *Pepper, are you okay?*

When Wickham turned away to board the *Sundew*, I snuck a glance behind me, hoping to see a familiar face, but there was no one in sight. I knew they were nearby, though. I gave a single nod, hoping that I'd be seen.

We have the location of the second set of books, said Oliver. *Now make an excuse and get out of there—we'll get them off the boat later.*

I hesitated. What if this was our best chance? What if he left in his boat and we lost the books?

And what if he came after the real Jane? By appearing as her, I'd put her in even more danger. I'd never met her, but I owed her. I had to neutralize him for her sake and ours.

Pepper, do not get on that boat with him.

Robert Wickham held out his hand to help me board. He looked like he was enjoying playing the spider to the fly.

I'd be alone. All alone, with this dangerous man, on a boat, on the water, with only a slim lifeline to my friends on shore, who couldn't follow me without raising suspicion—and the clock ticking until my disguise fell away. I'd seen the Godfather movies. I knew what happened when someone like that asked you to take a ride.

But water was my playground. My home.

My advantage.

I knew what I had to do.

I put on my most doe-eyed look and held out my hand.

We'd see who the real spider was.

37

I followed him through to the interior lounge.

"Can I get you a drink?"

I shook my head.

"Have a seat. I'll take us out so we can talk in complete privacy. The crew have the day off." He went on deck to cast off, then disappeared to the bridge.

When I was sure he had gone, I lifted the fire opal pendant. "Oliver?" I said, as quietly as possible. "Where exactly are the books?"

Pepper, you can't—

"I don't have time for you to tell me I can't."

The boat engine purred to life.

Interior bar, in the drawer.

I leaped up and lunged for the drawers, yanking them open one after the other. One held napkins, one held bar tools, and the last one held stationary. "There's nothing here!" Sweat broke out on my forehead.

Check for a false bottom, Oliver replied.

I shoved the napkins aside.

Nothing.

I pulled out the bar tools, lost my grip, and dropped them to the floor. They hit the plush carpet with a muffled thump.

Still nothing.

I hastily put the bar tools back in drawer number two and then opened the third drawer. Paper, pens, and envelopes filled the interior. I lifted them out and felt around the inside of the empty drawer.

There *was* something . . . a ridge? A catch?

The bottom panel of the drawer hinged upward, revealing a palm-sized hard drive. I removed it, replaced the false bottom, and dropped the stationary back inside. Drive in hand, I slid open the door and ran to the stern.

The marina receded into the distance. At the speed we were going, we'd be in the open ocean in minutes.

"Damn it," I said, striking the railing with my free hand. We were halfway out of the bay already. I could have jumped off at that point, even if it meant jumping in the water. But what would I do with the drive? And running away wouldn't necessarily get Wickham back to the marina, or the party, where we needed him to be.

"Oliver," I said, "I've got some time left on this face, right? And we can stay in touch?"

Your illusion spell will hold for a short while, and you and I can communicate indefinitely, said Oliver, *but Rose and Mrs. Millefleur will not be able to read his mind at this distance, even with you and the Eye in proximity.*

"I can handle it," I said. "I want to pick his brain. There's more to this than we thought. I'm almost positive Jane Wickham is a witch. And I'm sure she was afraid of him."

A momentary silence from Oliver, then: *We are coming after you just in case.*

"Stay back. I don't want him to notice anything."

As you say.

"Gotta go. He could be back at any second." I let the fire opal fall. Then I shoved the drive in my bag, hurried back inside, and settled on the couch where he'd left me.

Sure enough, when the boat had cleared the inlet and the close-to-shore waves, the engine turned off and Robert Wickham reappeared.

He remained standing, taking advantage of his relative height over me. "Have you given up that nasty habit of yours?"

What nasty habit did Jane have? Nose-picking? Shoplifting? It seemed safest to say yes, so I did.

He made a sound of derision and came closer.

Then he leaned down and *sniffed* my hair.

It was all I could do to sit still and not kick him in the store.

"Perhaps you're not lying," he said, straightening up. "It would explain why your voice sounds different." At least he managed to justify that without any help from me.

But what nasty habit changed your voice? Smoking? I mean, I didn't like smoking, but I didn't sniff people's *hair* to make my point.

"What made you change your mind?" he asked, studying my face.

This was deep water. Kind of ironic, because my mouth went dry. "You were right," I said, knowing that everyone likes to hear that, especially arrogant jerks.

"About what?"

Oh, crap. What did I say to that?

Everything, supplied Oliver's voice in my mind.

Thank God he could hear Wickham too. "Everything," I echoed.

Wickham chuckled and leaned on the bar, the master of his universe.

Except his universe was about to be minus one set of accounting books. Score one for the Ride-or-Die Witches.

Then, Oliver's voice again: *Ask him how you can be sure the witches will be safe.* Though he couldn't hear my thoughts, we were obviously thinking along the same lines.

"How do I know you won't use your list?"

"Are you still worrying your pretty little head about that?" He crossed his arms and gave me a twisted half-smile.

I nodded, widening my eyes to make myself look more fearful, but also concentrating my water magic on watching his pulse for signs of deception.

"It's still locked in the safe at Elozent."

His heartbeat remained steady.

"No other copies?"

"Knowledge is valuable. Why would I risk putting another copy out there?"

Pulse like a metronome. He wasn't lying.

Unfortunately, he was still talking. "And it will never see the light of day—unless you give me a reason." His expensive smile deserved to be cracked with a fist.

But I could play nice. "I won't, I promise." I cast my gaze down again. The move was ridiculous, yet he seemed to eat it up. "Robert?"

"Yes?"

"Could we go back to the party? Your friends could see us together—"

"I don't have friends, Jane. You know that."

"I really wanted to go . . ."

"It's not about what you want, is it? We can go back later." He said it lightly, but with clear satisfaction at being in control. He looked me up and down. "Why don't you freshen up while I take us out a little deeper?"

Like hell. Time to blow this pop stand. "Okay," I said, meekly.

The second he was gone, I ran to the stern. The hotel seemed so small in the distance. I could jump if I needed to—but that still wouldn't get him back to the marina and the regatta crowd.

The engine rumbled to life.

"He's heading farther out to sea. He's not coming back to the regatta," I said quietly, to Oliver.

Jump. We'll pick you up—we're close enough to get there in minutes, Oliver replied.

"No! He'll get away. And he might suspect something if he sees you coming too close." I glanced around the stern. I couldn't smash the engine with anything; it was mostly underwater, and Wickham would notice if I started hurling deck furniture at it.

The hotel continued to shrink. How far was he planning to go? I had the drive, but I had to stop the boat and get Wickham to willingly go back to the marina.

266

Through the fabric of my dress, I touched the pearl on my necklace, the Eye of the Elements, and the Key of Shadows. The Key was Lenore's way. It wouldn't do me any good here. What about the Eye? Extra power couldn't hurt. But what to use it for?

I had to do what I did best, and to do that, I needed to be in the water. I opened my bag and dumped the snack mix out of its double bag. Peanuts, pretzels, and Chex flew overboard to feed the fish. I shook out the crumbs as best I could and shoved the drive into the baggies, carefully pressing out air and sealing each one. Then I shoved the whole thing into the side of my bra, between the elastic bands.

I gripped the railing. Oh, this was not going to be easy. "Clove! Let's go, baby!"

Clove appeared in a spray of silver droplets. She hopped back and forth like a boxer getting ready for a fight.

I looked over my shoulder to make sure Wickham wasn't in sight. The coast was clear—he had to be at the helm while underway. I pulled off my stupid heels and threw them in the water, then angled myself as far away from the propeller as possible. "Count of three. One. Two. Three!"

We jumped. The sudden chill of the water nearly took my breath away as I sank below the waves. I kept my head and held my breath.

Time to change.

Turning into a mermaid was like making yourself see the hidden shape in a Magic Eye picture. Fix your focus just right, and everything snaps into place. I managed to tug my skirt north before the transformation so my tail didn't rip up the seams.

I felt heavier but stronger. My tail easily kept me in position despite the ocean current and the motion of the incoming waves. And, since I could stay underwater as long as I needed to, Wickham wouldn't be able to see me even if he went looking.

Clove swam in a slow circle around me, as steady as a small planet in orbit.

Now I had to stop the boat. I could see it heading away from me, out to sea, so I summoned my magic and created my own current to push against the boat. Great channels of magic-propelled water surged around me, slowing down Wickham's forward progress.

I pushed harder, dragging up every ounce of power, only to watch the boat chug against the current. I blasted out every drop of magic I could pull from the Eye of the Elements, too. Even that didn't help.

The engine was too powerful. I couldn't stop the *Sundew*.

I punched the water in frustration. I couldn't just let Wickham go. I had to get him back to the dock to finish the plan. My friends were counting on me.

Clove swam up and touched my hand with her paw.

Oh, Clove. Sweet baby girl. What should I do?

The *Sundew* continued to rumble into the distance.

Clove wiggled through the water on her back like she was floating down a lazy river.

Go with the flow.

Think big.

Goosebumps covered every inch of me that wasn't scales.

I closed my eyes, relaxed into a neutral floating position, and let my magic drift outward. The ocean surrounded me, cradled me, held me within its sparkling blue grasp. Into the blue magic I threaded my own, letting it weave through the waves like Clove.

Time slowed. My hands opened, palms up, as the pulse of the tide passed through me. Silver magic called to blue; blue magic responded to silver.

I was all things: woman, witch, and water.

This was what it was like to be one with the sea.

I could feel Clove turning somersaults in the water. I could feel the fish zipping by. Far away I could feel the Hipocampo as it made its way through the depths.

The magic connected me to the magical beast like a telephone line. I called.

It answered.

I didn't have to see to know it had changed direction and was now plunging in my direction. I pictured the *Sundew's* whirling propeller.

The Hipocampo's acknowledgment rattled wordlessly through our connection.

With my eyes still closed, I saw through the eyes of the Hipocampo as it raced to catch the *Sundew.* The hull grew larger as the Hipocampo got closer.

The Hipocampo veered astern and swirling bubbles from the wake clouded my vision. Its great crab leg rose up and up, taking aim—then came down and smashed into the propeller shaft with a sound like a cannon.

The broken propeller shaft hung askew, and the *Sundew* drifted to a halt.

38

I opened my eyes, slowly releasing my connection to the sea.

Ordinary sounds and sensations came back like someone had turned up a volume knob—including Oliver's voice, which rang with worry: *Pepper, are you there? Are you okay?*

Sure, I'm totally fine, I thought. *I was just temporarily one with the sea. No biggie.*

To my surprise, he answered as if he'd heard me. *One with the sea? We were afraid something had happened. You weren't answering, and then the Sundew stopped again.*

I blinked. The motion felt strange underwater. *Wait*, I replied, thinking back at him. *You can hear me think?*

Are you thinking? he replied.

Of course I am. I paused as the Hipocampo approached. Its large, horsey eyes crossed as Clove swam right up to its face. *I stopped the boat. Well, the Hipocampo did, really. Now we just have to get the boat in.*

Wickham is already calling for help on his radio, Oliver said. *There's an on-water assistance boat here for the regatta. They'll bring him in.*

Did he mention his missing wife?

A pause, while he presumably checked with whoever was monitoring the radio.

No, said Oliver.

Figured he would keep that to himself. I exhaled a bunch of bubbles. *Guess I'll start swimming back. No point in surfacing and giving the game away. Let him worry.*

Can you swim that far?

I smiled to myself. *With a tail, I can. But everyone's going to owe me a massage gift certificate to treat my sore muscles afterward.*

The Hipocampo nudged my shoulder with its nose. Clove had grabbed ahold of its head fin and was happily riding along.

Maybe I didn't need to exhaust myself, after all. I swam behind the Hipocampo's head and looked for a handhold.

Unfortunately, its neck was too big to hold, and its fins were too small and slippery. If only I had a rope.

A clicking sound alerted me to the presence of something large moving through the water nearby.

Dolphins! The sleek gray animals shot through the water around us. I reached out without thinking, hoping to pat their slippery skin, but they kept going—in the direction of the *Sundew*.

Clove, the Hipocampo, and I followed.

Three merpeople floated in the shadow beneath the boat. A flick of their tails, and they turned.

The Saltwater Queen's teeth glinted in a wide smile as her words carried straight to my mind. *Ah, water witch! This is your handiwork, I'll wager.*

Fisher swam forward and embraced me. *We heard your call, Lady Pepper. Are you well?*

The Sweetwater Queen, who had hung back, swam closer. Her eyes glowed green. *We will be pleased to drag this boat to the bottom of the sea, should you wish it.*

I shook my head. *I'm fine. It has to go back to the dock so we can finish him off,* I replied, hoping she didn't take it into her head to rip the boat apart anyway, just for fun.

At least, not yet.

The dolphins cavorted with the Hipocampo and Clove while Fisher and the queens peered up at the hull of the boat.

The Sweetwater Queen returned her gaze to me. *We are one, sea witch. What happens to you happens to us.*

An idea occurred to me. *Well, there might be one thing . . . I'd rather not have to swim a mile back to the marina. Could I catch a ride on your Hipocampo?*

The three of them traded amused looks.

Wait here, witch, said the Saltwater Queen. She and the Sweetwater Queen swam off rapidly together.

Fisher watched them go.

Are they still getting along? I asked.

It is not perfect, he replied, *but it is well.*

I elbowed him. *That's marriage, Fisher.*

The queens returned carrying ropes.

The Hipocampo swam over, carrying Clove, and allowed them to fasten the ropes like a harness. It only made two or three attempts to bite a chunk out of the reins.

We will accompany you, said the Sweetwater Queen.

Oh, no, that's not necessary— I started, but she didn't let me finish.

We did not ask your permission. Her green eyes flashed, then softened. *We will return you safely above.*

The Saltwater Queen laughed, and tousled her counterpart's hair. *Best not to argue with her when she's like this.*

The Sweetwater Queen looked royally indignant.

Fisher helped me get situated on the Hipocampo. I needed to communicate with Oliver to let him know I was on my way—but did he know already? Had I broadcast my conversation thoughts with Fisher and family? This telepathy stuff was complicated. Between magical artifacts and merpeople, who knew how it would all interact?

Only one way to find out.

I reached out tentatively, with an attempt to focus the communication and not blast it out to all the nearby merpeople: *Oliver?*

Yes, Pepper?

Did you hear any of that?

I did not, he replied.

Fisher, who was tightening a strap, did not look up.

The merpeople are giving me a ride back on the Hipocampo.

Ah, said Oliver. *Excellent plan. I will inform the others.* He paused. *The on-water assistance boat is about to arrive at your location.*

I looked up. Sure enough, the shadow of another hull drew closer from the west. It came alongside the *Sundew.* In a few minutes, the rescue boat engaged its engine, pulling the *Sundew* behind it.

The Hipocampo silently slid forward at a stately pace, towing the four of us and Clove fast enough to outpace the two boats. I used my water magic to create a friendly current that reduced the drag on all of us.

The dolphins flanked the Hipocampo like an honor guard, and we passed through the inlet and into the bay.

Where do you wish to go? asked Fisher.

Just get me near the marina. I'll swim in alone—I don't want you to get spotted in the shallow water.

When we stopped, Clove let go of the Hipocampo's head fin and swam back to meet me. Fisher and the two queens released their own harnesses and helped me get free of mine.

Go, said the Sweetwater Queen. *Your enemy approaches.*

I seized her hands, which seemed to startle her. *Thank you.* I let go and took the Saltwater Queen's hands next. *Thank you.* I faced Fisher, who seized me in a big hug.

Fare you well, Lady Pepper.

I swam toward the docks alone, dodging the boats and pilings, looking for a secluded spot to surface. A cautious peek above the water revealed no one in sight. I swam to a ladder and concentrated on exchanging my tail for legs. Then I tugged my dress down over my newly un-scaled hips and thighs, hooked my foot over the lowest rung, and pulled myself up. I climbed up to the dock and stood for a moment, the weathered wood rough on my feet, and squeezed excess water from my hair.

I crouched by the edge of the dock and peered down into the water. The reflection revealed my own face. "Hello, me!" I said—in my own voice, hooray!—then I stood and straightened out my dress, which had gotten twisted, and made sure the bagged hard drive was still securely tucked in the side of my bra. *I'm here*, I said silently to Oliver.

We're docking ahead of the Sundew, he replied. *Westernmost dock.*

I hurried to meet them.

When the *Tranquil Holiday* slid into view, I realized I'd never in my life been so happy to see a damn boat.

Luella threw her arms up in the air. "Pepper!" She and Rose scrambled down as soon as the boat was docked. Oliver and Raphael followed them down.

"We were so worried," said Rose. "That man's mind . . ." She shuddered. "Ugh. I need a shower."

"Me too," I said, picking a piece of seaweed off my dress. "Come on—let's get out of sight before the *Sundew* docks. He shouldn't see us hanging around."

There was a small building nearby about the size of a gardening shed. It floated right off one of the docks, and had a large cage mounted to the front of it, containing a blue-and-yellow macaw. The parrot squawked "Hello!" as the five of us hurried behind the building.

I peeked around the corner.

The rescue boat released the *Sundew*, and it floated the rest of the way into the dock where it could be secured.

"Where are your mom and Queenie and Mrs. Millefleur?" I asked Luella.

"Up at the party," said Luella. "Should I tell them to get the press in place?"

"Yes." I removed the fire opal necklace and the Eye of the Elements and passed them over to Rose. "Rose, get ready to set the spell on him so he can see the familiars." I gauged the distance from the *Sundew* to the party. "Oliver, Raphael, join the party crowd. Luella, Rose, and I will chase him up there. Hit him with the big guns."

Oliver nodded.

"You got it," said Raphael.

They took off.

"Who's a pretty boy?" squawked the parrot.

Rose, meanwhile, was ignoring the bird, murmuring to herself, and rubbing her thumb over the Eye. Bits of magic zipped away from her like silver embers.

"He's not getting off the *Sundew*," said Luella.

I nudged Rose. "Did you get the spell on him?"

She nodded.

"We gotta chase him off, then." My heartbeat sped up as a new wave of adrenaline kicked in.

"I'll go first," said Luella. She summoned Zephyr. The two of them looked around the corner. Luella gave Zephyr's ears an affectionate ruffle, then sent her off with a quiet "Go!"

Zephyr bounded away.

"Ooh, la, la!" squawked the parrot, with a French accent.

The white dog jumped to the deck of the *Sundew*, where Wickham was pacing, cell phone in hand.

A growl rose from the boat. Wickham started, then backpedaled away from the dog toward the bow. He tripped and lost hold of his phone, which tumbled overboard and landed in the water. "Nice doggie," he said, clambering onto one of the outdoor couches.

The growl turned into a vicious-sounding snarl. Zephyr leaped to the couch, barking wildly, sending Wickham running for the nearest hull door.

Rose, still concentrating, murmured Horatio's name.

Horatio sprinted forward, let loose an ungodly yowl, and launched himself at Wickham's calf.

Wickham cried out as sharp feline teeth sank home.

"Oh, that *had* to hurt," I said. "Let's bring it home, Clove baby."

Clove appeared in a sparkling splash of silver magic, ready and raring to go.

Horatio dashed to the side, leaving the way clear.

My sweet little otter darted between Wickham's feet, causing him to stumble, then scrambled up the back of his pants leg with an alarming series of peeps like a malfunctioning fire alarm. Then she seized his belt and sank her teeth into his rear.

Wickham howled and flapped his arms uselessly as Clove hung on and the other two familiars herded him in the direction of the crowd above the marina.

Rose, Luella, and I crept out of our hiding place and followed.

"Help!" he called, staggering across the wide lawn. "Help me!"

Having gotten him into position, Clove dismounted with an impossible-looking backflip. It was all I could do not to rush forward and hug her—but this wasn't over yet.

The three familiars circled Wickham with as much menace as a cat, a dog, and an otter could manage.

Wickham backpedaled away from what no one else could see. "Get away from me!"

At the sound of shouting, the closest people turned their attention to him.

Including a hotel security guard.

And not just any security guard—*my* hotel security guard.

At the same time, Mrs. Millefleur appeared at the edge of the lawn with a group of the press. The journalists lifted their cameras and microphones in the direction of the commotion.

"Sir," said the security guard, recognition dawning on his face, "I think I'm going to have to ask you to leave—"

But Raphael's raccoon familiar, Princess, had stealthily run up behind Wickham. She launched herself upward and swiftly climbed to his shoulders, where she put both paws over his eyes.

Wickham spun in dizzy circles, scattering nearby partygoers. "Get it off! Get it off!"

Princess appeared to be having a great time. She bounced on his shoulders like a seasoned horse-rider. The other familiars ran circles around the two of them.

"Ride 'em horsey!" said Luella, with quiet delight.

Then, as if at some pre-arranged signal, Princess jumped down and scampered away with the others. They lined the edge of the lawn like spectators. Mama's familiar, Crow, AKA Midnight, turned a lazy circle in the air above. All was quiet but for the sound of Wickham trying to catch his breath.

A great and shaggy brown bear stepped onto the lawn. It laid its deep brown gaze on Robert Wickham and let out a heart-vibrating rumble.

Wickham turned to run but scarcely made it two steps before Arthur was on him. The brown bear knocked him to the grass as easily as a child bats a balloon.

He tried to curl up into a ball, but the bear's paw kept him in place as Arthur lowered his muzzle and snapped sharp teeth in Wickham's face.

At last, Wickham just screamed incoherently.

"Ah, music," said Rose.

With one final snap, and a snort that sounded very much like a chuckle, Arthur released him and lumbered away. Clove and Princess clambered up for a ride on his back, Horatio and Zephyr walked alongside. They'd done their part like champions.

Rose let go of the Eye of the Elements, and the bits of silver magic faded away.

Robert Wickham got to his hands and knees, then pushed himself to his feet. His hair was wild. Grass stains marred his khaki pants. He'd lost a shoe somewhere along the way. His gaze swept the perimeter of the lawn and landed on Mrs. Millefleur.

His face twisted and reddened. "You," he said, pointing unsteadily toward Mrs. Millefleur. "You did this." He swung around, taking in Mama and Queenie across the lawn. "You're all a bunch of *witches*!"

"That's enough, *sir*," said the security guard, taking him by the arm.

Wickham shook him off. "They're all witches! All of them!" He stormed toward Mama and Queenie. He swung his arm in an accusing gesture that knocked off Mama's little blue hat. "Look at her. She's a witch!"

Mama and Queenie clutched at each other as if they were two helpless old ladies. Of course, they were nothing of the sort. Either one of them could have flattened him—but that bit of playacting quickly turned the mood of the crowd.

Several partygoers pushed forward, boxing him in. The security guard closed in, too, while the cameras ate up every second.

He lurched away from his pursuers, but stumbled to halt in front of me. Dumbfounded, he took in my appearance from head to bare feet. Confusion seemed to paralyze him just long enough for the security guard and the helpful regatta-goers to surround him again and hold him fast.

I didn't smoke, but at that moment, I wished I did—so I could blow it right in his face. Instead, I draped my arms over my friends' shoulders. "Get bent, you pile of walking garbage."

Mrs. Millefleur approached, impeccable in her formal regatta attire, trailed by a gaggle of journalists and camerapeople.

At the sight of her, Robert Wickham strained at the grip of the people holding him back. "I'll kill you," he said.

"I believe this is Robert Wickham, disgraced CEO of Elozent Industries," she announced, her voice clear and loud enough to carry to the spectators who had whipped out their own phones to video the scene. A ghost of a smile flickered over her face. "What a story this will be."

39

They wouldn't even let me set up my own wedding arch.

Rose and Luella shoved my board into my hands and pointed to the admittedly awesome-looking surf. "Go," said Rose. "You'll only be in the way."

I squawked in protest. "I can decorate stuff!"

"Don't make her hypnotize you." Luella gave me a hip bump. "March."

Thwarted, I crossed the fine, cool sand and waded into the breaking waves. The vow renewal would be totally informal, but my friends had insisted on crafting the perfect arch as a backdrop.

Who was I to stop them?

I slid into the water's embrace and paddled out. The rising sun glazed the foamy surf with orange highlights. Onshore, Luella and Rose assembled the arch and started attaching bits of stuff to it. Something white. Something green. Grass? Too far away to tell.

I went in search of the next wave.

By the time I'd ridden a handful more, a few more figures were moving around on the beach. Oliver and Raphael were setting up white folding chairs. Luella's mother and Queenie appeared to be wrestling with some sort of aisle runner that kept trying to blow away in the wind. Mama solved it by calming the air with great silver swirls of magic.

In the distance, Pete, Rocky, and Kevin made their way down the boardwalk stairs. The boys wore tie-dye t-shirts and bright swim trunks. Pete wore a crisp straw fedora over one of his vintage-style short-sleeve buttoned shirts and a pair of linen board shorts. He had enough fashion sense for the both of us.

I flipped my wet curls out of my face and smiled. Hair products? Saltwater and sea breeze. Outfit? Cute floral rash guard and coordinating swim shorts. Just how I liked it.

I readied myself to ride my last wave in—and it was a big one. I was speeding not only toward the beach but a new phase of life. Older, wiser, more powerful. Cool as hell.

The wave delivered me to shore.

Pete and the kids were already down in the sand, building a castle. My husband got up and opened his arms wide.

"Ah, ah, ah!" called Mama, from where she and Queenie were adding weights to the runner. "No huggin' and kissin' till the ceremony's done."

"Aw, man," I said.

"We'll make up for it," said Pete, sneaking in a side hug.

I returned the hug, then crouched next to Rocky and Kevin. "How's the sand castle going?"

Kevin pointed at a hand-dripped turret. "I'm making it look like the one at the hotel. See?"

"We need flags," added Rocky, with a serious look.

"We'll see what we can do about that," said Pete.

I patted the kids on the back and stood. A clinking sound caught my ear, and I turned to find Luella and Rose adjusting strands of seashells that hung from the arch.

"They can't be so low or they'll hit someone in the head," said Luella.

"That's probably good luck," countered Rose.

I moved closer. Three simple wooden beams created the shape of an oversized doorway. White cloth wound around the top and sides, fluttering in the breeze. Palm fronds and sprays of cream-colored flowers fanned around the corners next to accents of driftwood branches. The shells clinked together like wind chimes. "Ooh, pretty," I said.

Luella beamed, and Rose offered one of her more rare smiles.

I looked to the boardwalk, where a swirling cloud of something caught my eye. For a moment, I thought it might be magic—but it was only a woman in a hoodie, her face obscured, vaping into the morning breeze.

Mrs. Millefleur came down the stairs next. I don't know how she managed to walk across the beach in heels, but she did. She greeted me with a nod, from a distance, then pulled Luella's mother aside to say something in her ear.

"Looks like we have plenty of something old and something new, darling," said Queenie, coming up behind me. "And you've had the something blue all along," she finished, her gaze turning to the waves.

"I already gave back the something borrowed," I replied. My hand went to where my black pearl rested on my chest. Where the Key, the Eye, and the fire opal had rested, too. Mrs. Millefleur had taken the Eye of the Elements for safe-keeping. Rose had the fire opal. The Key had been returned to Lenore, who took it with her to Miami to make sure a copy of the Elozent books got into the right hands.

A dozen yards from shore, three swimmers popped up out of nowhere: Fisher, the Saltwater Queen, and the Sweetwater Queen.

Fisher waded out of the water. He had on Pete's trunks and the "I Went to Sparkle Beach and All I Got Was This T-Shirt" top.

I was a little worried the queens wouldn't wear enough clothing—seaweed and flowers don't cover much—but they emerged, barefoot, arm in arm, draped in gauzy layers that trailed into the water. In a merge of their usual styles, the Saltwater Queen wore some flowers in her hair; a few shells had been added to the locks of her companion.

When all of our attending family members had arrived, the guests settled into the white chairs facing the arch, the ocean, and us. In the front row, Kevin and Rocky toed the sand and looked anxious to hit the water as soon as possible.

Queenie unboxed a corsage and slid it onto my wrist, and Raphael helped Pete with a matching boutonniere.

Then Pete and I walked down the aisle and faced each other, a little awkward, a little excited, not too different from when we had actually gotten married.

He took my hands. "Pepper, you're the person for me. Always have been. Always will be. I'm honored to be your husband now and forever. You're not just the best mother and wife anyone could ask for; you're the best person I've ever met. I promise to spend the rest of my life telling you so, and trying to be worthy of you." Then he reached into his pocket and pulled out a small velvet box.

My jaw dropped. "What in the—"

He smiled. "I know we said we wouldn't do rings," he said, opening the box, "but I couldn't help myself."

A gold ring set with a black-and-green pearl nestled within. A pair of tiny gold dolphins wrapped around the setting. "Oh, Pete," I said, as he slid the ring onto my right-hand ring finger. I meant to say more, but the words tangled on my tongue. Instead I threw my arms around him and hugged him.

Everyone cheered and clapped.

Pete chuckled as I released him. "For a water witch, you sure are a ball of fire. I love you." He turned to the crowd. "And—Fisher? Do you think maybe I could have my trunks back?"

Everyone laughed.

Fisher sprang to his feet. "Most assuredly," he said, fumbling with the front drawstring.

"Not *now*, Fisher," I added.

"Oh! My apologies, Lady Pepper." He made a small bow and sat.

My turn. I took a breath to steady myself. "I'm not really good at making speeches—"

"You can do it, girl!" called Luella's mother.

I could do it—especially with a little help. I pictured Clove. She appeared at the far end of the aisle in a splash of silver magic, and hopped down the aisle to the arch. She took a position next to me and nuzzled my calf with her whiskery face.

My emotional support otter.

"Pete," I said, looking him in the eye, "I wouldn't have anyone else crew this boat with me. You're the one I always want by my side, whether it's calm or stormy. You're a great dad to Kevin and Rocky, you always make me smile—and hey, you're pretty damn sexy, too."

He laughed.

"Now kiss me, Mr. Monaco!"

He did. And it was a kiss as good as all our years together. After, we smiled at each other, and there were feelings in that moment that words hadn't yet been invented to express.

"And now I'm hungry," I said, with a wave of my hand, the one with the pearl ring. "Let's have cake!"

A cheer of approval went up from everyone, even Mrs. Millefleur. Luella unboxed the cake—a whimsical design with pale blue and green icing, sugar shells, and fresh flowers—and cut slices for everyone. The boys hurried to finish theirs so they could go play, but the rest of us took our time giving the vanilla and chocolate layers the attention they deserved.

While everyone else socialized, the mermaid queens slipped into the ocean together, their gauzy wraps trailing through the water. Fisher followed them in.

Suddenly, the nearby waves flickered with a blue-green glow, visible even under the strong light of the sun. The glow strengthened, growing and spreading, until it dazzled the waves for hundreds of feet in every direction.

"Does bioluminescence happen during the day?" asked Pete.

"It does today," said Queenie. She smiled.

Kevin and Rocky whooped, ran into the shallows, and began splashing each other with the glowing water.

The adults followed, gathering at the edge of the surf to marvel at the radiant waves.

Luella, Rose, and I waded farther out. We laughed as the bright glow swirled around our legs and grabbed hands when a bigger wave threatened to bowl us over.

Clove swam around and between us, tumbling through the waves as if they were a playground made just for her.

"Come on," said Luella, over the roar of the crashing surf. "Let's do our thing. On three." She held out her hand, palm down. "One."

"Two," said Rose, adding her hand to Luella's.

I put my hand over theirs. "Three!"

"Ride-or-Die Witches!" we cried.

Clove surfaced and added her own *peep* like an exclamation point.

Whatever happened, we had each other.

I looked over my shoulder. Pete had joined the kids' splash fight. He looked up, caught my gaze, and gave a happy wave of his hand before rejoining the battle.

On the horizon, dolphins leaped out of the water. The merpeople royal family was nowhere to be seen, although a brief flick of a tail appeared above the waves—along with the Sweetwater Queen's voice in my mind, saying, *We sank the boat for you, water witch. He deserved it*, followed by her light, bubbling laughter.

We watched the dolphins until the luminous blue-green glow faded. Then we waded toward the beach and made our way ashore.

Even though there was a splash fight to win, leftover cake to eat, and the best friends and family any witch could ask for waiting for me, I couldn't help turning back to the sea for one last look.

A silver-finned horse's head peeked out of the water. The Hipocampo snorted and tossed its head as if inviting me to come back. I blew it a kiss in return—a promise—and it wiggled its fins in satisfaction before sinking quietly into the sea.

Our adventure had only begun.

Find out where it all started.
Get the Midlife Elementals prequel!

* 9 7 8 1 7 3 4 5 1 4 4 9 0 *